A-TEAM III: WHEN YOU COMIN' BACK, RANGE RIDER?

'Get me the A-Team!'

As if in response to the barked command, Colonel Roderick Decker squinted through the sights of his automatic rifle and squeezed the trigger with obvious glee. A full clip of ammo slammed forcefully into the inert form of a suspended dummy hanging from the framework of the military firing range. The dummy did a dance, jerking wildly from the impact of the bullets, bleeding cotton batting from its pulverised heart. The anatomical bullseye was no longer visible, save for a few tattered shreds of crimson cloth dangling freely amidst the batting.

'Now, what was that you were saying? Something about the A-Team, sir?'

Also available:
THE A-TEAM
THE A-TEAM II: SMALL BUT DEADLY WARS

THE A-TEAM III: WHEN YOU COMIN' BACK, RANGE RIDER?

A novel by
Charles Heath

Based on the television series 'The A-Team'
Created by Frank Lupo & Stephen J. Cannell
Adapted from the episode 'When You Comin' Back, Range Rider?'
Written by Frank Lupo

A TARGET BOOK
published by
the Paperback Division of
W.H. ALLEN & Co. Ltd

A Target Book
Published in 1984
by the Paperback Division of
W.H. Allen & Co. Ltd
A Howard and Wyndham Company
44 Hill Street, London W1X 8LB

Typeset by Phoenix Photosetting, Chatham
Printed and bound in Great Britain by
Cox & Wyman Ltd, Reading

ISBN 0 426 19756 9

PROLOGUE

There were tall cottonwoods scattered about the Arizona plains, their light green leaves rustling in clusters at the end of thickly twisted limbs; and rock formations rose in errant patterns beneath the midday sun, filled with shadow and contour. But the most overwhelming feature of the landscape was neither tree nor stone. It was the grass that commanded one's attention and inspired a sense of awe. Months before, an abundance of winter and spring rain had made the grass grow as it had seldom grown before, tall and broadbladed, and a shade of deep green that brought to mind the emerald hills of Ireland. But once the rains had stopped, it was only a matter of time before the water-rich soil began to dry under the constant beating of the sun. As spring gave way to summer, the grass changed colour, and now the plains looked as if they had been spun from gold. For as far as the eye could see, the rolling terrain was a blanket of gold upon which the trees and rock formations were mere accents. A soft wind stirred the grasses, making them undulate like the amber waves that had inspired the opening lines of *America the Beautiful*. The whole setting spoke of idyllic serenity, the sort of place one might come to with nothing more than a picnic basket, camera, and a few hours to spend with a loved one or close friend.

Then the horses came.

Out they thundered from behind the rocks, where they had been grazing in seclusion only moments before. They were mustangs, wild and free-spirited, descendants from the days when the Great Plains were in Spanish hands. Their short ears were pricked back as they pounded their hooves on the parched ground, trampling the grasses in their way. Fear was in their eyes, and the fear had been put there by man.

As the many-coloured steeds raced across the open plain, three jeeps rolled out from the rocks in pursuit, splitting off on separate courses in hopes of encircling the herd and keeping them together. While the three drivers concentrated on the way before them, the men riding with them fired rifles over the heads of the horses to keep them moving and communicated back and forth by way of walkie-talkies. Phil Stryker was in charge of the operation, riding shotgun in the lead jeep. He was weatherbeaten from his sunbleached hair to his ruddy, wrinkle-etched skin, and wore denim that had been equally battered by the elements. Stubble covered his chin and he looked as if he hadn't slept since the last time he'd shaved. As he surveyed the fleeing mustangs, he shouted orders into his walkie-talkie, leaving one hand free to keep his Stetson from popping off his head each time the jeep bounded over a rise or dip in the land.

'Get 'em up over there, Flint! Bring 'em round! This load of glue ain't gettin' away!'

Setting the walkie-talkie down, Stryker snatched up his rifle and let out a whoop as he fired a shot into the air.

'Hey, boss, ya better aim higher or yer gonna nail one of them horses 'tween the eyes!' the driver exclaimed.

'Don't you worry none about my aim, Eddie,' Stryker advised. 'You just make sure we stay hot on them until we got 'em where we want 'em. I'll have plenty of time to plug 'em, then. I ain't gonna do it now, you can count on that!'

As Stryker's men were rounding the horses closer together, competing their rifle fire against the hoofbeats to see which could make the loudest disruption, a solitary figure watched on from the cover of an outcropping of rock that afforded an unobstructed view of the plain below. Daniel Running Bear had heard rumours of rustling on the land between his reservation and the large cattle ranches to the east, but this was the first time he'd witnessed the crime as it was taking place. He wasn't sure which emotion had the tightest grip on his heart, his empathy for the mustangs or his loathing for the men who were chasing them. What he did know was that he couldn't stand by and let the round-up continue.

Rising from his crouch, Daniel scampered deftly from rock to rock until he reached the knoll where his own horse was tethered to an old tree. The steed was fidgeting in place, pawing its front hooves impatiently in the dirt as it whinnied.

'That's all right, Stone,' he calmed the grey horse as he untied the reins and bounded into the saddle. 'We'll see to your cousins soon enough. Let's go!'

Stone cantered down the sloping incline of the knoll, then broke into a gallop as it circled around the rock formation and took to the plains. Securing himself in the saddle, Daniel took up his rifle and held it out to his side as he rode towards the clearing where Stryker and the others had managed to gather the mustangs into a manageable circle. Having forsaken their firearms for lariats, the riders were standing up in the jeeps and lassoing the more rowdy of the horses. Stryker was overseeing things with a grin of satisfaction, waving his arms to direct the last phase of the round-up.

'Nice goin', boys!' he shouted to the others. 'Now let's just mosey these varmints back to Mister Carter's and get ourselves some of them nice bonus bucks, eh?'

'Yeah!' Eddie Dexter howled next to Stryker. 'Let's do it!'

The others were in the midst of voicing their affirmation when a gunshot rang through the air and echoed off the rock facing of the nearest escarpment. Before the rustlers had a chance to react, the mustangs were once again unnerved and acting on their first impulse. Some reared and neighed with terror as they smote the air with their hooves, while others bolted for the nearest opening, mindless of the lassoes around their necks. Several of Stryker's men were jerked from their jeeps before they were able to let go of their lariats and avoid being dragged behind the fleeing stallions.

'What the hell?!' Stryker roared, looking over his shoulder at the source of the explosion that had thwarted his day's work. Seeing the lone Indian riding headlong towards them, he yelled at his driver, 'Turn this thing around, Dexter! I want that man for myself, the bastard!'

As the other man struggled to keep the horses from getting away, Daniel levelled his rifle at their jeeps and fired off a quick round of shots. One managed to puncture a front tyre of the closest vehicle, forcing it to veer so sharply to one side that the other jeep slammed into it and became suddenly airborne, sending the men in both jeeps flying into the surrounding grass.

The stampeding horses were heading off in all directions, and as Dexter was trying to turn his jeep around, he and Stryker found themselves cringing to avoid flying hooves as several of the mustangs leapt over the front hood in their quest for freedom. The frenzy of activity was raising great clouds of dust that further added to the confusion. Dexter stopped his jeep and tried to blink away the loose dirt flying in his face.

'Hang on!' Stryker urged, holding a hand over his eyebrows to deflect the duststorm. 'Hang on!'

'It's some crazy Injun, man!' Dexter hooted, getting a faint glimpse of Daniel as he rode past the jeep and began screaming loudly and waving his arms to further spook the horses. He continued firing his rifle into the air, too, and was so absorbed in what he was doing that he neglected to keep an eye on his enraged adversaries. It wasn't until a bullet whistled past his ear that he hazarded a glance back and saw that Dexter was bearing down on him in the jeep, with Stryker taking aim for another shot with his rifle. Daniel whipped his own rifle into firing position first, though, and sent his last bullet through the jeep's windshield. Dexter leaned away from the shattering glass and let up on the accelerator.

'Stay on him!' Stryker demanded.

'That Injun's nuts!' Dexter protested.

'He's also gonna be dead!' Stryker vowed, taking

another wild shot at Daniel. 'Now stay on him! Look, he's outta ammo! Come on, it's either his hide or yours, Dexter!'

As Dexter reluctantly took up the chase, Stryker used his last few shots trying to bring down Daniel, but the Indian's riding prowess proved to be better than the foreman's aim. Ducking from side to side, Daniel avoided the gunfire and at the same time guided his horse away from the stampeding mustangs and towards the nearby escarpment. The pitch of the rise was far too steep for the jeep to traverse, and Daniel felt sure that he would be able to elude the rustlers by riding back up to a higher elevation. Turning his back on the advancing jeep, he slapped the reins and dug his heels into the hindquarters of his horse, shouting, 'You can do it, Stone. Come on, you have to!'

Stone sought out the surest footing on the rugged incline, but the horse's progress was slowed down considerably, and Dexter was able to bring the jeep close enough for Stryker to stand up and artfully fling his lariat at the Indian. Stryker had won a fair share of rodeo ribbons for his rope-handling, and his expertise was rewarded when the wavering lasso swooped down neatly over Daniel's shoulders. Taken by surprise, Running Bear was being unceremoniously yanked off his horse before he had even begun to grab for the tightening loop of rope that had ensnared him. He landed hard and off-balance, stumbling back down the incline before coming to a halt a few yards from the jeep.

'Go, Stone!' he gasped as he tried to regain the wind that had been knocked out of him. His horse hesitated a moment, then clattered up the rise and vanished from sight before one of the men from the other jeeps could run over and draw bead on it with his rifle.

'Nice ropework, boss!' Dexter said, turning off the jeep and getting out. 'Want me to hog-tie him?'

Stryker nodded, giving the rope a sudden tug just as Daniel was getting to his feet. The Indian staggered back to the ground, scowling at his captors.

'You've got me, but the horses are free,' he gloated.

Stryker chuckled maliciously as he picked up the walkie-talkie. 'That rhymes real pretty-like, y'know. Hey, Dexter, looks like we caught ourselves a poet. Mebbe we ought to show him a line or two of our work. Know what I mean?'

'Yeah, I gotcha, boss!' Dexter took the rope from Stryker and tightened the bonds around Daniel, then shoved the prisoner downhill and behind the jeep. As he was tying the free end of the rope to the jeep's rear bumper, he chortled, 'Gonna teach you good. You cost me a tidy bonus, but it'll almost be worth it to see what we're gonna do to you!'

'And what do you think that will prove?' Daniel said, trying to keep his courage up. 'I'm not the only one out to stop you from what you're doing.'

'Once we've made an example outta you, I don't think we'll have to put up with anyone else playing hero,' Stryker told him. 'I don't know what it is you Indians are smoking in them peace pipes nowadays, Geronimo, but you are gonna be one sorry redskin.'

There was a garble of static on the speaker of the walkie-talkie, followed by a deep, sonorous voice that reeked of authority.

'Is that you, Stryker?'

'Yessir, Mister Carter,' Stryker replied. He paused to sigh, then delivered the bad news. 'The herd got away.'

'I thought you radioed before that you were chasin' them into the valley! How could they get out?'

'It was one of the Indians, Mister Carter. He just – '

'"One of the Indians"? Is that what you said, Stryker? One lousy Indian screwed up the whole crew of you?'

'I'm afraid so, sir,' Stryker said, making a face into the walkie-talkie that was a bit less polite than his banter. 'I'm sorry, Mister Carter. On the bright side, though, we got him.'

'Who? The Injun?'

'Yessir.' Stryker leered over his shoulder at Daniel, who was putting up a fight, leaning forward and butting

Dexter off his feet with his head. Before Running Bear could wriggle free of his bonds, though, another of the men came up behind him and knocked him out with a blow to the back of his head. The prisoner slumped to the dirt and didn't move further. 'Yessir,' Stryker repeated. 'We got him cold.'

'Well, send him back to his reservation,' Carter's voice snapped over the walkie-talkie, 'in a basket . . .'

'You got it, Mister Carter. We'll take care of him, then I'll bring the boys in. Next week we'll get those horses back, I promise.'

'That's what you promised today,' Carter reminded his foreman. 'What's this next week crap?'

'Well, we had a few problems with a couple of the jeeps,' Stryker said, looking past Daniel at the two crumpled heaps lying on their sides in the tall gold grass like downed hippos. 'Gonna need to take 'em into the shop.'

'You're the one who's going to have to be taken into the shop if things don't start changing for the better around here, Stryker. Do I make myself clear?'

'Yessir.'

'Good. Once you're back I want a full report on what happened. For now, take care of the Indian.'

'Will do.' Stryker set down the walkie-talkie and swore a stream of profanity under his breath, then grabbed his canteen from the back seat and bounded out of the jeep, moving around to where Daniel Running Bear was just coming back to his senses. Stryker poured water on Daniel's face, and when the Indian sputtered, he told him, 'You ruined my whole day, friend, so I'm gonna return the favour. Dexter, hit it!'

Dexter was back behind the wheel, and on Stryker's signal he started up the engine and drove off, dragging Daniel behind the jeep. The prisoner bounded roughly off the harsh terrain, groaning with each blow. As blackness began to creep over him, drowning out the jeers and howls of the men around him, Daniel clung to the one thought he hoped would pull him through the ordeal he was being subjected to.

Revenge.

ONE

'Get me the A-Team!'

As if in response to the barked command, Colonel Roderick Decker squinted through the sights of his automatic rifle and squeezed the trigger with obvious glee. A barrage of gunfire rattled through the afternoon air and a full clip of ammo slammed forcefully into the inert form of a suspended dummy hanging from the framework of the military firing range. The dummy did a dance, jerking wildly from the impact of the bullets, bleeding cotton batting from its pulverized heart. As the target continued to sway and shed, Decker slowly lowered his rifle and let a thin smile register his pleasure in the performance he'd just put on for his superior officer. He'd pumped so many of his bullets into the dummy's heart that the reddened outline that had distinguished the anatomical bullseye was no longer visible, save for a few tattered shreds of crimson cloth dangling freely amidst the batting.

'Nice shot, Colonel,' General Bullen conceded.

'Why, thank you, General,' Decker said, letting the smile grow on his face until it was on the verge of becoming a smirk. 'Now, what was that you were saying? Something about the A-Team, sir?'

Twenty years separated the two men, and they shared enough common attributes to give the illusion that they were father and son. Both had stocky frames of thick bone and conditioned muscle, and tanned skin that provided pronounced contrasts for their pale blue eyes. Decker was the younger of the two, and his hair was both darker and more in presence than the General's receding grey locks. There were more stars, stripes, and medals adorning

Bullen's uniform, as befit his rank, and yet he seemed to go out of his way not to appear condescending to the Colonel. If anything, he treated Decker as an equal, in deference to the Colonel's reputation. Word around the base was that if Roderick Decker was as interested in promotions as he was in being his own man, he could have been a general several times over. Decker himself seemed to be as aware of this as anyone, and the knowledge made him one of the most self-assured men General Bullen had ever dealt with. Bullen felt almost intimidated by Decker, seeing in the Colonel the embodiment of his innermost fantasies concerning the way he wished he could conduct himself. Bullen knew only too well that in most of his dealings he resorted to pulling rank in order to get his points across; he lacked Decker's ability to be matter-of-fact in a way that eliminated any need to bring a pecking order into consideration.

'Sir?' Decker asked, stirring Bullen from his thoughts.

'Oh, yes, yes, here . . .' The general held out a file to Decker. 'These men have been wanted for over ten years and it's time we closed the book on them once and for all.'

Decker ignored the file and busied himself with reloading his rifle. 'That case has been on the back-burner for years,' he muttered, letting contempt ride on his words. 'It's common knowledge Colonel Lynch has been waging his own little war – '

'Precisely,' Bullen interrupted. 'That's why Colonel Lynch is now out of the picture and this matter is hanging fire.'

'Lynch out of the picture?' Decker tried to make it sound like an innocent inquiry, but even Bullen could sniff out the sense of intrigue behind the colonel's comment.

'That's correct. Colonel Lynch is now behind a desk back in Washington, taking out his frustrations on paper clips and water coolers. It's what he's best at, really. This matter with the A-Team really should be in more competent hands.' Bullen eyed Decker knowingly.

'I can't argue with that, General,' Decker said, clamping an ammo clip onto his rifle. 'Tell me more.'

Flipping through the file, which contained, among other things, ten year old photos of Hannibal Smith, Templeton Peck, and Bosco Baracus, Bullen commented, 'These three soldiers were tried and convicted because of extreme political pressures of the time . . . something you should understand, Colonel.'

Decker met the general's grin with a light snort of amusement, then lowered his rifle and reached out for the file. Noting the dated mugshots, he said, 'I've seen newer photos of these guys. Smith and Peck look pretty much the same, but this Baracus guy's picked up a jewellery fetish over the years and he's got one weird haircut. Looks kinda like Sammy Davis Jr. on steroids, they tell me.'

The general indulged in a slight chuckle, then cleared his throat. 'Very good again, Colonel. I like that!'

'It's yours,' Decker deadpanned, turning to the thick pile of reports taking up most of the file.

'They were all but forgotten about within a couple of years of their escape from Fort Bragg,' the general said. 'But with Lynch constantly throwing balls down their alley, he's mushroomed this into what is viewed as an extremely embarrassing string of situations . . .'

Skimming through the file, it didn't take Decker long to find a prime example of what the general was talking about. 'December third, nineteen seventy-seven,' he read aloud, 'they relieved Colonel Lynch of one executive jet belonging to the military . . . two months later he lost five MP cars in a high-speed chase . . .'

'For which we had to make restitution to a number of innocent shop keepers whose store fronts were destroyed in the process, thanks to Lynch,' Bullen drawled. 'Last year, after we got ourselves some headlines for capturing the Team, they escaped a full security military installation – '

' – taking with them a military troop plane under Lynch's command,' Decker read. Closing the report, he shook his head and mumbled, 'It's enough to give the service a bad name.'

Bullen nodded gravely. A few yards down, another

officer had showed up and disrupted the silence with a volley of gunfire from his revolver. The general waited for the din to settle, then said, 'All in all, the A-Team has made a fine bunch of jackasses of all us, just like you say, Colonel.'

'Maybe we should do something about it, huh?'

'Not we, Colonel,' Bullen corrected, his blue eyes sparking with emotion, as they often did when he got around to giving orders. 'Not we. You. I want you to find the A-Team and bring them in.'

'Me, sir?' Decker asked innocently.

'Why not? After all, all during Nam you were our best troubleshooter. You were always the one we could count on . . .'

'Until extreme political pressures knocked the hat off my career and any possibility of furthering my rank,' Decker interjected sarcastically.

'That's all water over the dam, and you know it, Colonel,' Bullen insisted. 'These days you're the only one holding you back from rising up the ladder.'

'Oh, I don't know about that, General.' Decker turned away from Bullen a moment to shout a few words of encouragement to the other officer on the range, then looked back and said, 'What this all boils down to, if you ask me, is that the very methods that made me an . . . embarrassment, as I think I've heard you put it . . . it's those same methods that make me the man for this job, right? I wasn't good enough for stars back in Nam, but now you think a little flattery is all it takes to make me forget.'

'Now look here, Colonel, I'm not saying – '

'We both know what you're saying, General, so let's not dance once around the floor.' Decker handed the file back to Bullen. 'Everyone heard the reports that came back from Nam on these guys. I knew about 'em back then when we were only a few dozen miles away from each other. They're top-notch at what they do, because they're sharp, fast . . . and unorthodox. To catch men like this you have to play by their rules, which means there are none.'

While the general mulled over Decker's analysis of the

situation, the Colonel swung his rifle up to his shoulder and took aim on the dummy the third officer had been shooting at. The heart had been nicked only once, so the crimson target was clearly visible. Decker lined it up in his sights and proceeded to empty his rifle into the dummy, having as much success as he had with his own.

'Hey, Decker, leave something for us amateurs!' the other rifleman shouted.

'You had your chance,' Decker yelled back, flashing a grin. Turning to General Bullen, he lowered his voice. 'Okay, so what's the bottom line here?'

'What I'm interested in, Colonel, is the results,' Bullen replied, trying to match Decker's straightforwardness. 'I don't expect detailed reports on the whats, hows and whens of their apprehension. I just want it done. Erase this blot from our records and I will be pleased. In turn, many other people will be pleased. Come the time you decide you want to move up in the ranks, I'm sure no one would be standing in your way.'

'How sure?'

'Get the A-Team and you'll find out, Colonel.'

Decker quickly readied another round for the rifle, then told Bullen, 'Okay, general, you got yourself a deal. I'll get them for you. Count on it.'

'I am, Colonel. I am.'

Decker held the rifle out to General Bullen and asked, 'Care to?'

General Bullen took a step back, shaking his head. 'No, Colonel. That's all right. Perhaps another time.'

'Right,' Decker replied. This time, he let the smirk take over his face.

TWO

A thick batch of smog stew was brewing in the Los Angeles basin, colouring the air with tints of brown and green. The weather forecasters weren't holding out much hope for relief, either. If anything, they were predicting more heat and worsening conditions in the air quality. The beaches were crowded with souls looking to escape the onslaught, and those unable to make it to the coast tried to stay indoors near the air-conditioning vents. Tempers ran thin and highway shoulders were crowded with cars that had broken down under the oppressive heat. The whole city seemed to be in a foul mood, and the police were working overtime to keep crime from festering, as it invariably did under such circumstances.

Daniel Running Bear was no stranger to urban environments, but he always felt a sharp sense of alienation when venturing into a city after stays at the reservation, and LA struck him as particularly ominous, and only partly because of the weather. After leaving the bus station in the heart of downtown, he'd been subjected to haggard pan-handlers wanting dollars for inflated cups of coffee, leather-clad punksters who mistook him for lead singer of The Tommy Hawks, gang members who thought he'd strayed from his turf in the barrio and was looking for a fight, pamphlet peddling religious zealots wanting to save him by indoctrination into their quasi-mystic cult, and gay cruisers who assured him he'd look simply fabulous in a studded loincloth. By the time he'd reached his initial destination, a laundromat run by a certain Mr Lee, he was almost ready to turn around and head back for Arizona. Mr Lee did little to make Daniel feel as if he'd made the right decision in coming to LA in hopes of securing the services of the A-Team. After interrogating Daniel with a fusillade of questions couched in pseudo-Confucian gibberish, the inscrutable proprietor of the laundromat had informed the Indian that his best chance of getting directly in touch with the A-Team was to take a bus to the Wilshire business district and buy a hot dog from the street vendor at a corner park. Daniel had pressed for more details, but Mr Lee abruptly ended their conversation by ducking out the back door, moments before a potbellied Irishman strode into the laundromat and told Daniel he was Lee Bowman, owner of the shop.

Now it was almost three hours later, and Daniel had finally come up with the right bus connections to find himself on Wilshire Boulevard at the beginning of the business district. For the next half-hour, he searched for a corner park, at the same time avoiding the stares of businessmen sweltering in their three-piece suits as they talked shop on their way to, as they put it, do some lunch or take a meeting. Noticing that the ethnic makeup of those around him was widely varied, he began to realize that the attention he'd been drawing all morning probably had less to do with his native features than with the fact that those same features were mottled with welts and bruises he'd received during his torture at the hands of Phil Stryker and Eddie Dexter. He also had one arm in a cast and walked with a pronounced limp. All in all, though, he considered himself fortunate. If the rope that he'd been dragged behind the jeep by hadn't snapped after chaffing against the rocky terrain, he wouldn't have been able to make the frantic dash to his waiting horse that allowed him to escape an almost-certain death. A week after that incident, there were few parts of his body that didn't still throb with pain. The discomfort was an ongoing reminder of what he'd been through, and it served to keep up his determination to see that the treatment to both himself and the wild mustangs was avenged.

It was eleven o'clock when he finally came upon a swatch of landscaped greenery that fit the qualifications of being both a park and being located at the corner of Wilshire. Even more encouraging, there was a lone vendor fidgeting with his cart a few yards away. The man was bearded and stoop-shouldered, and the morning's heat kept his wire-rimmed bifocals constantly slipping down his nose. A sign on the side of his cart advertised his wares. As Daniel walked over, he noticed that one of the vendor's specialities was hot dogs.

'Morning,' Daniel said pleasantly, stopping alongside the cart.

'Mornin',' the vendor mumbled without looking up from his work. He opened a side panel and took a package of buns from the cart, then emptied them into a steamer. The aroma of tube steaks was just beginning to emanate from the stand, competing with that of pretzel dough.

'You're, um, the only hot dog vendor in this park?' Daniel asked hopefully.

'Don't see no other,' the vendor sniffed, pushing his glasses back up his nose before he started filling squeeze bottles of ketchup and mustard. 'And I won't. Got a contract with the city says that. This is my turf.'

'I see.' Daniel had hoped that his arrival would have been anticipated, but it seemed clear that if the vendor had anything to do with the A-Team, he wasn't about to divulge his connection, at least not without receiving some sort of password. Remembering Mr Lee's instructions, Daniel cleared his throat and asked, 'Uh, could I have a hot dog, please?'

'You kiddin'? Too early for hot dogs.' The vendor cupped his hand into a fist and coughed into it in a way that suggested he was stifling a burst of private laughter. Deciding to let Daniel in on the joke, he explained, 'I only got lukewarm dogs right now. Just fired up my burners, y'see . . . You want a warm dog?'

'Yeah, well . . . okay . . . whatever,' Daniel stammered, trying to not sound discouraged.

'You don't seem so sure of yourself, sonny.' The vendor extracted a handkerchief from his rear pocket and dabbed at the perspiration welling the grooves of his brow.

'There's a coffee shop right across the street, y'know. Got hot food there. Nice danish, decent donuts, some chili so hot it'll make this weather seem like winter. Real breakfast food. Oughta try there, mebbe.'

'No,' Daniel insisted. 'I'd like a hot dog . . . or a warm dog, if that's all you have.'

The vendor raised the lid of the steamer and peered inside, then shook his head and adjusted the temperature dial. 'Not even warm yet. Gimme a few seconds, though. I got it cranked up to overdrive. Get ya a warm one, but I gotta say, I never heard of anyone eatin' a hot dog at eleven a.m.'

'If that's the case, then why do you open this early?'

'Don't open up,' the vendor corrected. 'I fire up at eleven. Then I'm open by noon for the lunch crowd. Work from noon till four. Been doin' it for close on twenty-eight years. I'm a well established firm in these parts.'

'That's great,' Daniel said. 'Then maybe you know Mister Lee? Either works or owns a Chinese laundry down near the bus depot downtown?'

The vendor didn't react to the name. As he started salting his unbaked pretzels, he asked Daniel, 'This is a big town, sonny. I don't gotta go downtown to wash my clothes. Why should I know some guy there?'

'He told me to come down here and buy a hot dog.'

'Wish he'd told me,' the vendor grumbled. 'I'da told him to tell you not to come till noon. Fire up at eleven but the dogs aren't ready till noon.'

'Yeah, right.' Daniel adjusted his sling where it was biting into his shoulder and waited for the vendor to broach the subject of the A-Team, although he was beginning to think he either had the wrong man or else Mr. Lee had sent him on a fool's errand by way of telling him the Team wasn't interested in his situation. Before leaving, though, Daniel decided to try one more time. 'See, I kinda have this problem and . . . well, I got the impression from Mister Lee that you might be able to help me . . .'

The other man shrugged as he removed one of the

franks and mated it with the bun. 'Yeah, well, a job like this, you're kinda like the local bartender. Get to hear people's problems, help 'em out if I got some advice, sometimes just let 'em get it off their chests . . .'

Daniel sighed and ran his free hand through his hair. 'Well, thanks anyway,' he said, starting away. 'Sorry to bother you.'

'Hey, don't forget your dog,' the vendor said, swaddling the frank in a napkin. 'And I need eight bits for it. Buck-fifty.'

'Never mind, I lost my appetite . . .'

'I can't take it back,' the other man said, holding the dog out to Daniel. 'Health Department . . . they got codes about this kinda thing. Don't want to have to toss it away. People out there starvin' who'd love a lukewarm dog.'

Some of those people were visible in the background. A couple of transients were dozing in the shade and a lean pair of senior citizens glanced periodically at the vendor's cart between moves in their twelfth checker match of the morning. 'I guess you're right,' Daniel said, trading two dollar bills for the hot dog. 'Keep the change. By the way, do you know if there's another corner park on Wilshire?'

The vendor shook his head and began loading pretzels for baking. 'Nope. This here's prime turf, and it's mine. Have yerself a good day now, hear?'

'At the rate I'm going, I don't know if that's possible,' Daniel said bleakly. Heading off into the crowd of pedestrians, the Indian took a bite of the hot dog and made a sour face. As he raised the napkin to his lips to spit the meat out, he stopped. There was a message scrawled on the corner of the napkin.

'CORNER OF LAS PALMAS AND HOLLYWOOD BOULEVARD. TWO A.M. JUST WAIT.'

'What is this?' Daniel muttered aloud, glancing over his shoulder and seeing the vendor wheel his cart down a walkway bisecting the park. Stuffing the napkin in his shirt pocket and discarding the hot dog in the nearest trash can, Daniel headed back to the park, trying to keep an eye on the vendor through the crowd. By the time he reached the belt of thick shrubs the other man had rolled his cart behind, though, he'd lost him. The unattended cart stood near the base of a towering palm tree, but the vendor was nowhere to be seen. Daniel took a close look at the transients sleeping nearby and the elderly men at the checker game, but none of them looked remotely similar to the man who'd given him the hot dog. It was then that Daniel recalled that when he'd first been told about the A-Team by a fellow tribesman at the reservation who'd served with the Team in Nam, his friend had said that two of the men, Hannibal Smith and Templeton Peck, were masters of disguise as well as experts in weapons and battle tactics. It all began to make sense. In fact, the more he concentrated on his encounters with Mr Lee and the vendor, the more he became convinced that the two men had been one and the same. Facial discrepancies aside, both had silverish hair and blue eyes and spoke with deep resonant voices. From what his friend had told him about the Team, he came to the conclusion that he'd already met twice with the group's leader, Hannibal Smith.

'He's testing me somehow,' Daniel whispered to himself as he left the park area. Taking the napkin out and rereading the message, he added, 'If that's the case, hopefully this means I've passed . . .'

THREE

A tourist's jaunt down Hollywood Boulevard invariably begins or ends a few blocks west of the corner of Las Palmas, where the Chinese Theatre, one of Tinseltown's more venerable treasures, stands in quasi-Oriental splendour, a pagoda-styled building with sculpted dragons, stately spires, and ski-slope roofs framing the large, glowing marquee touting this season's likeliest blockbuster. Legendary as the movie theatre itself is, the institution has earned an even greater measure of fame with its opulent courtyard, which sports countless slabs of cement containing imprints left by matinee idols of past and present. During the day, numerous booths also clutter the courtyard, enticing the nonstop glut of curiosity seekers pouring out of tourist buses with everything from souvenir postcards to discount tickets to a wax museum down the block that depicts what the superstars of the silver screen might look like if they'd been reincarnated as department store mannequins.

But it was night now, and the last of the tourist buses had departed hours ago. The theatre was now the site of that dying phenomenon, the gala premiere. Instead of buses, it was sleek limousines that rolled up to the kerb and opened their doors to disgorge an endless parade of would-be celebrities for a walk down the red carpet to the theatre lobby. A sizeable crowd of onlookers had gathered with the local paparazzi, hoping for a glimpse of next year's Oscar winners, and a pair of giant klieg lights shot broad beams of light up at the sky and sliced through the smog as if trying to let some cool air seep down from the heavens and give the city some relief from the heat wave. The beautiful people put on the shows of their lives trying to look comfortable in their tuxedoes and evening gowns, but few of them lingered to bask in the adulation of admirers. The majority chose to hurry towards the lobby and the welcome gush of chilled, conditioned air. As they moved inside, the invited guests walked under the gleaming marquee, which exclaimed to the world that the reason for tonight's festivities was the opening night of a film called 'WINE FOR BREAKFAST'.

Instead of popcorn and Juicy Fruit, the snack fare in the lobby consisted of a full buffet being served up by one of the more prestigious local caterers. Caviar and canapes abounded, and spiked punch was served from a bathtub-sized punchbowl in which the ice-carved likeness of a mermaid bobbed and melted like the wicked witch in 'The Wizard of Oz'. Vacuous conversation, a speciality of those gathered for the opening, reverberated through the lobby, giving off an aura of excitement. There was considerable activity near the rest-rooms, where men and women went in looking slightly on edge and came out looking vibrant-eyed and ready for anything, sniffing through their stimulated nostrils like bloodhounds on the scent of fresh prey.

Presiding over the evening's activities was none other than Templeton Peck, decked out in a tailored tux and flushed with a reddish tan he'd picked up earlier that afternoon at the beach. Composed and oozing with panache, he held court with a handful of industry climbers who were ever-nodding and smiling with their mouths closed, the better to keep from drooling in anticipation of scoring a few choice connections by the time the night was through. At Peck's side was a statuesque blonde who looked as if she'd been blown-up and painted specially for the occasion. Her evening gown was low-cut in a way that seemed to defy gravity, and her exposed cleavage was like a magnet to the iron filing pupils of the men around her.

'I'm tellin' ya, boobie,' Peck was intoning as he waved a celery stick for emphasis, 'we shoot all three pictures at once, get the two sequels in the can while we're shooting the first one, then we just coast to the bank, knee-deep in green, am I right?'

'It sounds great, Jer,' said a short, owlish man standing directly across from Peck. Not wanting to come off as a mere yes-man, he hesitated a moment, then qualified, 'If the first one opens big, of course.'

'I hear you, Mick, I hear you. Believe me, we're talkin' major box office business here,' Peck enthused. He chomped down the stick of celery, then drained the Bloody Mary it'd come with before linking arms with his overendowed sidekick. 'Hey, Gretel, babe . . . you've met the Mick, haven't you?'

'Ja,' Gretel said with an accent as thick as her mascara, offering Mick a slight bow that almost liberated her breasts from their meagre confinement. 'Ja.'

Mick's tinted glasses allowed him a moment to ogle Gretel's glandscape before making eye contact and gushing, 'I'm real happy the Jer could fly you over from Germany for this premiere. I really am.'

'Ja,' Gretel cawed, clinging tighter to Peck's arm and baring a toothy smile that would have made a piranha blush. 'Ja.'

'Ja,' Peck seconded playfully, placing one hand over Gretel's as he stared past his entourage at the rest of the throng crowding the lobby. 'I think this is gonna be a big night. Everyone who's anyone has turned out.'

One of the everyone who's anyone Templeton Peck hadn't counted on showing up for the premiere was seated in the front of a nondescript sedan parked across the street from the theatre, in front of the Roosevelt Hotel.

Colonel Decker puffed contemplatively on a briar pipe and stared through its bluish curls of rising smoke at the courtyard, where disappointed fans were beginning to trickle away, having seen the last of the limousines pull away from the kerb. Behind the wheel of the sedan was a uniformed lieutenant by the name of Crane, which also was an apt description of his appearance. Tall and gangly, Crane had a long neck with an Adam's apple that protruded like a burrowing mole in a cartoon, and a beak-like nose situated atop a moustache the colour of carrots. His eyes were small and pale, constantly darting to take in the entire periphery of his surroundings. When his gaze lighted upon the dashboard, he whispered, 'The screening's scheduled to start in fifteen minutes, Colonel.'

Decker took a last draw off his pipe, then set it in the ashtray. 'Let's get ready to move. He'll have too much advantage in a darkened theatre.' Going to his side, the colonel withdrew a .45 automatic. He quickly checked the clip to make sure it was full before ramming it back into the butt of the pistol. 'Are our men inside ready?'

'I'm sure they are,' Crane responded.

In addition to the caterers, there were a handful of waiters hovering about, passing out complimentary champagne, refilling hors d'oeuvres trays, and plucking up cigars and other burning objects dropped on the carpet by guests too engrossed in talk of points and sushi to bother with ashtrays. One waiter, with the build of an off-season linebacker, glanced up at the wall clock, then drifted away from the punch bowl, circling around the clot of people gathered around Peck, who was playing out his role of megabuck producer to the hilt.

'. . . and Gretel here does a beautiful love scene . . . the nudity is tastefully done.' Face looked over at his protege and Gretel blushed on cue. He winked at her, then continued pitching, 'Really. I mean, an easy cable sale . . .'

The waiter tapped Peck on the shoulder. 'A call for you, Mister Jameson.'

'For me?' Peck tried to wave the waiter away as if he were a pesky fly. 'Take a message . . .'

The waiter moved closer to Peck and pointed something hard into the back of Templeton's ribcage. Leaning forward, he whispered in Peck's ear, 'You don't want these people to know you're a conman with the A-Team instead of a bigshot producer, do you, "Jameson"?'

Without missing a beat, Peck smiled indulgently at his audience and removed Gretel's hand from his arm. ''Scuse me a minute, troupers . . . long distance. I may have that spot in Cannes I was hoping for . . .'

With the waiter escorting him from close behind, Face started for the hallway leading to the manager's office.

Gretel broke away from the others, but Peck turned to her and said, 'You stay here and keep the Mick company . . . the Jer'll be back in a sec.'

Peck was accosted by more well-wishers on the way to the office, and each time he tried to start up a conversation, the waiter jabbed his ribs and forced him to move on. Finally they had shaken the rest of the group and the waiter reached past Peck to open the office door, whispering, 'Inside, ace.'

'How nice,' Peck said, stepping into the office, which was small and cluttered with theatrical business paraphernalia. 'I was wondering how I was going to manage to get away from that mob out there. Very thoughtful of you to help. Now, if you'll just get that gun barrel out of my abdomen so I can digest my . . .'

Peck's voice trailed off as the waiter stepped away from him and withdrew the champagne bottle that had been masquerading as the business end of a pistol. The waiter himself had been in disguise, and when he yanked off the black wig and false moustache, Peck let out a gasp that was equal parts relief and aggravation.

'Hannibal! What is this?' he demanded. 'What's going on here?'

'I think that's my question,' Hannibal replied, unbuttoning his collar and loosening his bow tie. 'I'm supposed to be meeting our client in a couple hours and I've been trying to reach you all day.'

'You should have left a message at the Beverley Hills office,' Peck retorted.

'I didn't know we had one,' Hannibal said, reaching to his back pocket for the most recent edition of the industry trade paper. 'What do you call this?'

Peck stared at the headline, 'JERRY JAMESON IMPORTS FINE WINE' and shrugged.

'Well?' Hannibal asked. 'What's the scoop, Jer old boy?'

'A bad picture,' Peck sniffed, eyeing the photograph accompanying the story. 'Looks like they caught me comin' out of La Serre Thursday. Sheesh, you'd think they'd hire professional photographers for front page stories at least.'

'You've lost your drive wheel, you know that?' Hannibal said, tossing the paper on the desk. 'What do you think you're doing?'

'I've decided to produce. Miracle Films.' Peck pulled a business card out of his shirt pocket and handed it to Hannibal, pointing to the inscription beneath his name and reading, '"If it's a good film, it's a Miracle."'

Hannibal shook his head and muttered, 'You're nuts. Who'd you scam into footing the bill for this extravaganza? I've seen inaugural balls that cost less than this.'

'Nice, huh?' Peck picked up the bottle of champagne Hannibal had discarded and started opening it. 'Dom Perignon. The Monsignor always told me that anything worth doing is worth doing right. Don't you agree?'

'You haven't answered my question, Face. How'd you scam up the cash for this shindig?'

'That's just it, Hannibal, in Hollywood, when you get someone to pay the freight, you're not scammin', you're producin'.' Peck popped the bottle and poured out doses of the champagne into a pair of coffee mugs sitting on the desk. 'And there's tons of guys out there who don't know what to do with their money who are always looking for ways to get into the biz. The glamour, the broads, the parties . . . you know, people who like to have fun and rub elbows with the in-crowd. They run this town these days, you know.'

Peck handed Hannibal one of the mugs and raised his for a toast. Hannibal finally cracked a smile and chinked mugs with Face. 'I've got to hand it to you, you're good, Peck. I've been waiting twenty years to have someone throw a party like this for me. How do you do it?'

Peck sampled the champagne, then said, 'I needed a showpiece, so I scrambled around, looking for any piece of junk I could get my hands on. I find this little number, made by a couple film students for ten grand. I dub it in German, than have it subtitled back into English and tell everyone I brought it from overseas, made by some genius working around government oppression. The critics see that and right away you're looking down the business end of a good review. I'll clean up on the art house circuit.'

'"Wine for Breakfast"?' Hannibal said sceptically.

'That's one of the little finesse touches,' Face confided. 'You give it a lousy title and say it doesn't translate well from the original. Gives it that aura of enigma. Nonsense in the clothes of profundity. You know the maxim for foreign films, "If I can't figure it out it must be good."'

Hannibal sipped his champagne slowly, then laughed, 'Maybe you oughta run this number on some of those turkeys I did stunt work in. I could earn some residuals and we wouldn't have to break our necks playing *Mission: Impossible* all the time.'

'Better yet, before you so rudely interrupted me, I was shining on some distro bigwigs with the majors to see if one of them would coffee up big numbers to carry "Wine for Breakfast".'

'Excuse me, Face, but what language is this you're speaking?'

'Hollywood lunchese.'

'Well, let's either stick to English or else I'm gonna need a Berlitz guide, okay?' Hannibal finished his drink and set it aside. 'How'd you get your paws on Helga out in the lobby?'

'Gretel,' Face corrected. 'She's out of the screen actor's local. She was the best looking thing in the picture so I hunted her up. Found her waiting tables at Charley's Charbroiler on the Strip. But forget this chump change. I have a script I want you to read that's gonna be my first statewide production . . . "The Beast of the Yellow Night".'

'Some guy in an ape suit roaming through the smog?' Hannibal guessed.

'Close,' Peck said, 'only it's not an ape suit. I see something with scales, fire through the nose, a fetish for women who do nylon commercials on the tube.'

'Seems to me I remember seeing that one on the late show last week,' Hannibal cracked.

Peck ignored his partner's sarcasm. 'And guess who's gonna play the Beast?'

Hannibal pointed at his sternum, then shook his head

firmly. 'No way. I've already done my creature feature. This is too small a town for me to get typecast so early in my career.'

'Baloney. By the time I'm done they're gonna have your claw prints in the cement out front.'

'And they're gonna have you behind bars.' Hannibal snatched up the trade paper and pointed at Peck's picture. 'At least when I take an alias I change my looks, Face Man. You've got a mugshot at the Pentagon that looks just like this pic here.'

'C'mon, Hannibal, you don't think Lynch reads the film trades, do you?' Peck refilled their cups, then started for the door. 'Hey, whaddya say, long as you're here you can scrape the rest of the putty off your face and meet some of the guys . . .'

'I've got a client I have to meet,' Hannibal reminded him. 'I've already run him through Mister Lee and the hot dog vendor and I'm gonna snap him up and take the case. I came by to tell you to meet B.A. at the hospital and spring Murdock. Amy'll meet us at the warehouse. We're leaving this smog behind and taking our sinuses to Arizona!'

'Aw . . . I can't,' Face complained. 'Not tonight!'

'It has to be tonight,' Hannibal maintained, leading Face out of the office. The lobby was thinning out as people began to head into the theatre. Gretel was still holding Mick and the other men at bay with her anatomical charm.

'But I'm just about to turn these guys for a couple mil,' Face said. 'You trying to tell me you've got a job that'll net more than that? Look, I can't douse the houselight and leave these guys with a box of popcorn and wet dreams of Gretel to remember me by.'

'Face,' Hannibal said. 'You're not George Lucas yet. We need the job and this guy, Daniel Running Bear, needs help. Go get Murdock. And keep your head down. Lynch could be right outside at this moment.'

FOUR

Colonel Lynch was a few thousand miles away, tossing in his sleep as he struggled with nightmares recounting the many botched opportunities to capture the A-Team that had led to his reassignment to the limbo of deskwork. His replacement, however, was in the process of confirming Hannibal's apprehensions. Emerging from his sedan, Colonel Decker was joined by Lieutenant Crane and two other uniformed officers who had been waiting in an unmarked van a few parking spaces away. Together the four men paced across Hollywood Boulevard with brisk precision, weapons at the ready. There were a few stragglers milling about the courtyard, checking their hand and footprints against those of the stars or else waiting to see if they could slip inside once the lobby had cleared for the start of the movie. One middle-aged couple were taking each other's picture in front of the box office when they saw the approaching officers.

'Look, Al!' the woman pointed. 'Isn't that George Peppard?'

The husband lowered his camera and scrutinized Colonel Decker as the others hurried past. 'Naw, Uly, it ain't him.'

'Are you sure? Take his picture just in case!'

'I'm down to my last shot, Uly,' Al protested. 'I ain't gonna waste it on some wild goose chase. Get back over by the box office!'

But Uly wasn't listening. Clopping awkwardly on her high-heels, she hurried across the courtyard and intercepted Decker before he could reach the entrance to the lobby. 'Excuse me, but aren't you George Peppard?'

she asked, tilting her horn-rimmed glasses to focus in on the man she'd cornered.

'Outta my way, lady!' Decker snapped gruffly, easing the woman to one side as he glanced up at the roof of the Chinese Theatre, where several more officers were crouched behind sculpted outcroppings. 'Watch the exits!' he shouted. 'We're going in!'

'Well, you obviously can't be George Peppard,' the woman huffed. 'He's a gentleman. Wait, I know! You're Don Rickles! I get it! You're dressed up like that as part of your routine – '

'Excuse us, ma'am,' Lieutenant Crane said as he pulled the woman away from the door, 'but we're on official business. We're not actors. This is the real thing. Be nice and get lost before the bullets start flying, all right?'

'Uly, do like the man says and get over here,' her husband beckoned impatiently. 'I told you security was tight around a big deal like this. There's no way we're gonna get inside.'

As Uly dejectedly headed back to the box office, Colonel Decker counted quietly to three, then led the three other officers into the lobby. They charged in with the fierce determination of an anti-terrorist unit, quickly breaking out in separate directions, weapons levelled at those around them as Decker howled, 'Military police! Everyone drop!'

There were only a dozen people still in the lobby, including Hannibal and Peck. As the others slumped to the carpet with fear, Peck dived behind the buffet table while Hannibal put his trust in what little makeup he was wearing and discreetly grabbed an unopened bottle of champagne from the table next to him before lowering himself to the floor.

Decker had been scanning faces from the moment they'd burst into the lobby, and he'd identified Peck just before he'd moved behind the buffet table. Pointing his .45 at his unseen quarry, Decker commanded, 'Give it up, Peck!'

When there was no response, Decker signalled to Crane

and the two of them waded through the cowering guests toward the table, both their guns trained on where Peck had last been seen.

'His name's not Peck,' Gretel said, glancing up at the two officers as they walked past her. She'd lost her accent in the excitement. 'He's Jerry Jameson, a famous – '

'Put a lid on it, bimbo,' Decker snarled down at her. 'By any other name, he's still the same meat to me. Isn't that right, Face Man? Why not make it easy on everyone and show yourself? I'll take you dead or alive; it's all the same to me . . .'

As Decker closed in on one side of the table, Crane broke away and moved to block off any possible escape the other way. He'd only taken a couple steps when there was a loud, sudden bang. Crane let out a cry of pain, dropping his gun as he reflexively reached for his face, where he'd just been hit by a speeding champagne cork. The dropped gun fired, sending an errant shot up into the acoustic tiles that lined the ceiling. Not sure what had happened, Decker crouched down and crabbed to the cover of the portable bar. The other two officers likewise scrambled for the protection of the nearest obstacle. Taking advantage of the moment's confusion, Hannibal rolled away the foaming bottle of champagne and rushed over to the buffet table, where Face had stood up and was now wrestling with the gigantic punch bowl.

'Give me a hand, Hannibal!'

'This is hardly the proper way to serve punch, Face,' Hannibal wisecracked, helping Peck to tilt the bowl until the icy mermaid was in a position to dive headlong to the floor, where she shattered into fragments amidst the downed guests.

'Let's get out of here,' Face said, heading for the nearest exit. He pushed through the door, which promptly swung full-force into the face of an officer who was about to open it from the other side. Stunned, the officer reeled backwards, leaving the way clear for Hannibal and Face to bolt past him and down the adjacent hallway before Decker and the others could negotiate their way through the maze of now-frantic guests and random icecubes. The lobby was quickly reduced to a madhouse of slapstick frenzy as soldiers slipped and collided with each other or with the men and women who were straggling to their feet, wondering aloud if the ongoing shenanigans around them were part of a carefully orchestrated publicity stunt instigated by the mysterious Jerry Jameson.

When Hannibal Peck saw more officers emerging from stairwells down the hall, they quickly ducked into the first room on their right, which happened to be filled with women powdering the insides and outsides of their noses. There was an abrupt chorus of shrieks and screams as the two men raced past, heading for the window facing the side alley.

'Just passing through, ladies,' Hannibal assured them.

While Hannibal was prying the window open, Face paused to catch his breath, warning the women, 'Watch it when you leave here, 'cause there's some army boys outside on a three day pass and looking to make up for lost time.'

'Come on!' Hannibal said, squeezing through the opening in the rest room. As Face came to join him, he eased himself out to the point where he could drop to the side alley. Peck was halfway out the window when Gretel burst into the rest room and called out to him, 'You'll call me?'

'First chance I get,' Face promised. 'Right now, I'm going location hunting.'

Gretel was suddenly tugged away from the doorway to make room for Decker, who raised his gun and aimed out the window. Before he could get a shot off, one of the women next to him hauled off and clobbered him with her purse. 'Of all the nerve!' she cried indignantly, giving the colonel a second swat for good measure.

Outside, Hannibal and Face hurried down the alley to the main street, where Al and Uly were having their pictures taken in front of an impressive Ferrari, putting on the airs of celebrity for their photographer, a parking attendant they'd bribed with ten dollars to shoot them before taking the car to the parking lot in back. As the attendant was flashing the snapshot, Hannibal motioned for Face to wait in the shadows while he went to the kerb to see about securing some transportation.

'Hey, ace,' Hannibal chided the attendant, a gum-chewing young man with a pencil-thin moustache. 'Mister Jameson's been hunting high and low for you!'

'For me?' the attendant said, handing the camera back to Al. 'I've been right here.'

Hannibal pointed down the alley. 'Well, you should be back there. There's a real fender-bender in the lot . . .'

'Funny, I didn't hear anything . . .'

'You were probably too busy chewing gum and glomming tips from the tourists. Now get!'

The attendant blew a bubble in a lame gesture of defiance, then jogged down the alley, leaving the Ferrari at the kerb. Grinning, Hannibal circled around and got in behind the wheel.

'Hey, wait!' Uly cried out to him. 'Aren't you George Peppard?'

'Come off it, Uly,' her husband said, grabbing her by the arm and leading her away, 'You got George Peppard on the brain. Let's get you outta the heat before you end up with permanent brain damage!'

'What are you getting at?' Uly retorted.

As the couple headed off to continue their argument, Hannibal started up the Ferrari. Peck broke clear of the shadows in front of the theatre and hurried to the car, getting in just as Hannibal was gunning the accelerator.

'I always wanted to test drive one of these things, Face. What'll it be? The hills or the straightaway?'

Peck noticed several officers rushing out of the theatre courtyard and into the street behind them, blocking off their likeliest escape route. 'I think the hills would be a nice change of pace, Hannibal.'

'You got it.'

As Hannibal pulled out into the street and took the first turn leading up into the Hollywood Hills, Decker finally made it out of the theatre and rushed down the alley in time to see the tail-lights of the Ferrari vanishing around the corner.

'That's them!' one of the officers in the street called out as he and two others piled into one of the military's sedans. The colonel ran over to get into the car with them.

'Get after them, and hurry!' Decker roared. 'The one who catches them gets to keep his rank!'

The military received their first break of the evening when Hannibal encountered a full lane of traffic stalled for a stoplight just shy of the hills. By the time the Ferrari had managed to break free of the congestion and enter the rolling side roads, Decker's sedan was in close pursuit, taking advantage of the vehicle's surplus horse-power to keep pace with Hannibal's driving.

Hannibal grit his teeth and worked the clutch relentlessly, going through gear changes every few seconds to try to widen the distance between them and their pursuers. Glancing at the dash tacometer, he told Face, 'Someone oughta tell the guy who owns this that he's got a shimmy at eighty-five . . .'

'By the time you're through, he's gonna need a whole new clutch,' Face said, clawing at his seatbelt in hopes of securing himself against what seemed to be an eventual collision. 'You know, it isn't Lynch who's after us this time. They got somebody else I never saw before.'

'Relief pitcher, I guess,' Hannibal said, cruising tightly around a corner that led past a row of lavish homes tucked up against the hillside. Checking the rear-view mirror and spotting the headlights of Decker's sedan rounding the bend. 'Whoever it is, he's got one reckless driver working for him. Could mean trouble.'

'If we don't shake 'em soon, there's bound to be choppers tailing us from above,' Face said. 'I think we should double back and get back in building country.'

'I'll give it a shot.' Hannibal eased up slightly on the gas, and the other sedan moved in closer towards them. As the Ferrari hurtled through a dimly lit intersection, Hannibal suddenly stood on the brakes, skidding the sports car into a sidesweep that almost ended with contact against the corner kerb. At the last second, though, Hannibal was able to bring the vehicle under control and negotiate the hairpin turn leading back down into the city. Decker's sedan sped a few dozen yards past the intersection before the driver's reflexes enabled him to adjust to Hannibal's manoeuvre and change course. With the few seconds he'd gained, Hannibal was able to elude a second sedan taking up the chase and speed downhill to where the roadway widened and the traffic was more of a factor. Once again, stoplights proved to be Hannibal's foil, and by the time they were coming back onto Hollywood Boulevard, the gap had been closed by Decker's men.

'Any other suggestions?' Hannibal asked Face.

'How about that parking structure?' Face said.

'Are you kidding? It'd be a dead end!'

'We don't have much choice, Hannibal. You checked your gas lately?'

Hannibal inspected the instrument panel and saw the fuel gauge leaning on empty. 'Just our luck. Well, here goes . . .'

Hannibal screeched his brakes and pulled sharply into the multi-level garage, slowing down as they came alongside the booth housing a uniformed guard who manned the gate.

'Excuse me, sir, but could you state your – '

'He'll take care of it,' Hannibal explained, hooking his left thumb over his shoulder, indicating the sedan that had just pulled in behind him.

'But, sir, I – '

Hannibal left the guard in mid-sentence, racing under the wooden arm that was being lowered to block his access to the parking structure. Decker's sedan didn't stop, either, and splinters went flying as it crashed through the barrier and followed the Ferrari up the rampway leading to the second level.

In all, the garage had eight levels. Hannibal was able to gradually increase the distance between the Ferrari and the sedan with each rise, although it was at the expense of

Face's internal equilibrium. Peck was beginning to look like a man in the throes of seasickness.

'Hannibal, I'm gonna die if we don't run outta levels and shake these guys soon.'

Hannibal ignored Face as he drove on, eyeing the parked vehicles flanking him on either side. 'Where are the car buffs around here?'

'What are you talking about, Hannibal?'

'Aha! Bingo!' Hannibal said, suddenly swerving into a parking space next to a parked sports car with a tarpaulin over it. Jumping out of the car, he grabbed the tarp and shouted, 'Hurry, Face, they'll be here any second!'

It was a Porsche that had been covered by the tarp, and when Decker's sedan came rolling by a few seconds later, it was the Porsche they saw instead of the veiled Ferrari, under which Hannibal and Face cringed, hoping their ploy would be successful.

'Where the hell are they!' Decker shouted as the sedan sped by.

'This is the top level,' his driver told him. 'They must have started down.'

'Then get down after them! I want those guys in my hands!'

Once the military vehicle had descended to the next level, both Hannibal and Face raised the sides of the tarp enough for them to roll down their windows and breathe some fresh air.

'Well, so much for delays,' Hannibal said cheerfully, pulling a cigar from his pocket and lighting it with the dash lighter. 'I hope our client won't give up waiting for us.'

'And to think I almost gave this up in favour of producing,' Face said bleakly.

'Cheer up, Face,' Hannibal said, blowing smoke in Peck's direction. 'This new guy who's after us looks like he's gonna be more fun than Lynch. I just love a close call.'

Peck opened his door and leaned out, moaning, 'I think I'm gonna be sick.'

FIVE

As Decker's sedan shrieked its way down the exit ramps of the parking structure without encountering so much as a glimpse of the Ferrari, the Colonel pounded his fist on the dashboard and shouted, 'Faster, damn it!'

'If I push this sucker any harder they'll have to scrape it off the walls with a spatula . . . sir!' the driver shot back without taking his eyes off the ever-changing view before him. As it was, the tyres were already screaming with protest each time the car took a corner, shedding still another thin skin of rubber onto the concrete.

'If they shake us, soldier, it's you they'll be scraping off the walls with a spatula!' Decker spat. 'Now get a move on!'

'But, sir – '

'You have your orders!'

As they descended still another level without spotting the Ferrari, the third officer in the back seat gripped the armrest for support and ventured, 'Colonel, I think we passed them somehow. I haven't heard another car for some time now.'

Over the whining of the tyres, Decker shouted, 'There could be a jetliner flying through here and we wouldn't be able to hear it. Driver, I want that pedal to the metal, right now!'

Swallowing hard, the driver clenched his fingers around the steering until his knuckles were white, then slowly coaxed the accelerator closer to the floorboard. The sedan picked up speed, taking each successive corner wider than the last, until, three levels up from the ground floor, the laws of physics caught up with the vehicle and it scraped its passenger side against a guard railing. A shower of sparks flew from the moulding strip as the car carommed wildly off the railing. It took all the driver's expertise to keep from spinning out and crashing into a row of parked vehicles. He braked hard and veered sharply to one side as all three men braced themselves for what they felt would be an inevitable collision. The driver closed his eyes and muttered a quick prayer. It was apparently answered, because when he opened his eyes, he saw that the sedan had come to a stop only a few feet shy of the garage elevators. Letting out a breath of relief, he glanced over at Decker. The Colonel's face was tightened into a mask without expression, and the driver couldn't tell what was going through the officer's mind.

'Sir . . . ?' he queried feebly. 'I'm sorry, but this car just isn't made for this kind of driving.'

Decker didn't answer at first. He was staring out the windshield, his eyes on the numbers posted above the doors of the elevator, indicating the eight levels of the parking structure. The numbers lit up to show the direction the elevator was heading. At the moment it was going up, having just passed the floor they were on. Snapping out of his seeming trance, Decker suddenly spun about in his seat and told the officer in the back, 'Get out and take the stairs down. Guard the exit and don't let them get past you.'

'But, sir, if they're already ahead of us, by the time I run down there – '

'They aren't ahead of us!' Decker shouted without bothering to acknowledge that it was the third officer who'd initially reached that conclusion. 'Just get out and get going!'

'Yes, sir!'

As the man was getting out of the back seat, Decker told him, 'Station yourself near the elevators when you get down there. I think they're making their break on foot!'

The officer nodded, withdrawing a revolver from his holster as he bounded down the staircase next to the elevators.

‘What do we do, sir?’ the driver asked.

‘We wait.’

And wait they did, sitting in the front seat of the sedan and staring at the elevators. When the lights above the doors showed that the elevator was stopping at the eighth floor, Decker whipped out his gun and took aim at the push button used to summon the elevator. The moment the indicator light began to move from eight to seven, he emptied his .45 into the control button and surrounding plate. As he’d hoped, at least one of the bullets ploughed through some essential wiring, and while both the eight and seven numerals above the elevator doors were more lit than the others, the glow was faint and erratic.

‘All right!’ Decker shouted. ‘We got ’em trapped between floors! Let’s go back to the top and get ’em!’

Crumpled as the one side of the car was, it still ran, and the driver started back up the various levels of the garage, slowing down each time it passed the elevators so that Decker could make sure they were still inoperable. Reaching the top floor, they passed by the vacated Ferrari and the recovered Porsche.

‘So that’s how they did it,’ Decker mused. ‘Clever, Smith, but not clever enough.’

The driver stopped alongside the eighth floor elevator and turned off the ignition. As he was reaching for his gun, Decker told him, ‘Give me that. You get the tyre iron out of the trunk so we can pry these doors open.’

Decker took the other officer’s gun and they both got out of the car. Once the driver had found the crowbar and brought it over to the elevators, the two of them put their weight into using it to jimmy the doors wide enough apart to squeeze through. Decker leaned into the cavity and glanced down. As expected, he saw the roof of the elevator car a few yards down.

‘Right where we want them!’ Decker gloated, a savage gleam in his eyes.

‘What now?’ the driver asked.

‘I think I’ll drop in and say hi.’ Decker assumed a paratrooper’s stance, crouching at the edge of the opening and judging the distance to the trap door in the roof of the elevator car. 'Geronimooooooo!'

The colonel flung himself into the cavity and dropped feet-first, holding his gun above his head. He made no effort to cushion his fall, and when his full weight came in contact with the thin layer of sheet metal and acoustical tile marking the trap door, he crashed through effortlessly and landed inside the elevator car with the nimbleness of a gymnast. The element of surprise was in his favour, and the occupants of the elevator were too stunned to do anything but stare with wonder at the armed officer who had suddenly appeared in their midst. Unfortunately for Decker, however, those occupants weren't Hannibal Smith and Templeton Peck, but a pair of teenagers who had been taking advantage of the elevator foul-up to engage in a little adventurous romancing. When they broke from their embrace and let out cries of shock, the boy's left fingers were snagged inside his girlfriend's sweater, where they had been attempting the insurmountable task of single-handedly unsnapping the backside of a bra.

'Hey, we weren't doing anything!' he gasped, trying to work his incriminating hand free. 'Honest!'

'We just stumbled into each other, that's all,' the girl collaborated. 'Don't hurt us! We're just kids!'

Decker glared at the youths as he pointed his gun away from them. 'There were two guys up on the eighth floor, one of them in a tuxedo and the other in a waiter's outfit. Did you see them?'

Both teenagers nodded nervously. 'I saw 'em switching a car tarp from a Ferrari to a Porsche,' the boy said, 'Then they started off down the stairs.'

'The stairs? This is the eighth floor! Why the hell did they take the stairs?'

The youths looked at one another guiltily, then the girl confessed, 'Because we told them the elevators were out of order. It was just a joke . . .'

'Yeah, you two are a real pair of comedians,' Decker grumbled. He holstered his gun, then pulled himself back up through the shattered trap door.

'Hey, mister, is this elevator going to start up again?' the young man called out.

'No, it's out of order,' Decker told them. 'Funny, huh?'

The other officer was still up at the eighth floor, and he reached down to give Decker a hand, saying, 'False alarm?'

Once he was back out of the elevator, Decker nodded. 'They took the stairs down.'

'Then we'll still get them,' the driver said. 'There's no way they could have reached the lower floors before we did on foot. Our man down there will be ready for them.'

'I'm not taking any chances,' Decker said, going over to the car and getting on the two-way radio. When he reached a dispatcher, he said, 'This is Colonel Decker. I want all available units at Hollywood and Edmund, on the double. There's a parking garage here, and I want everyone on the lookout for Smith and Peck. They're on foot and you all know what they look like!'

As Decker was putting the radio mike back, the driver said, 'Should we head back down?'

'You should, and take it slow,' Decker told him. 'I'm taking the steps, just in case they're hiding out there.'

'Gotcha, sir.'

As the driver got back into the sedan and drove off, Decker took to the stairwell, once again getting out his gun. He made his way down swiftly but silently, keeping an ear open for any suspicious sounds. Halfway down, he came across a discovery that made his heart sink. There was a pedestrian crosswalk extending from the fourth floor of the parking structure to the upper level of a hotel across the alley. As soon as he saw it, Decker knew that had to be the way Hannibal and Face had fled. Rather than continuing the rest of the way down the steps, he took the crosswalk and entered the hotel. This late at night there was no one about, and it wasn't until he reached the downstairs lobby that he came across anybody. A sprightly-looking woman in her mid-thirties was at the registration desk, whiling away her shift on a Rubik's cube.

'Military police,' Decker identified himself as he approached the desk, startling the woman.

'Yes?' she said anxiously, cupping her hands around the cube. 'Can I help you?'

Decker gave Hannibal's and Peck's descriptions and asked if she'd seen either one of them.

'There was someone in a tuxedo,' she admitted. 'He borrowed the phone for a second, then rushed out, in a real hurry.'

'Which phone?'

'This one,' she said, pointing to the receiver on her desk. 'He said he'd lost his wallet so he didn't have a dime and, well, I guess I'm a sucker for a pretty face.'

'What'd he say?' Decker interrogated. 'Who did he talk to?'

'Someone whose name was just initials. A.P., P.A., something like that.'

'B.A.,' Decker guessed.

'Yes, that's it!' the clerk said. 'He asked this B.A. to pick him up a few blocks from here, right away!'

'And you didn't see any trace of this waiter guy,' Decker asked. When the woman shook her head, the colonel tersely thanked her, then rushed out of the lobby, reaching the entrance to the parking structure in time to catch his two officers in mid-argument with the irate security guard near the splintered gate arm. Surmising that none of the men had seen Hannibal or Peck, Decker ignored the confrontation and went straight to the sedan, picking up the radio.

'This is Colonel Decker again,' he said, 'Recheck the files for a make on that van B.A. Baracus drives and then have everyone on their way here keep an eye open for it.'

'We're one step ahead of you,' the dispatcher replied over the speaker. 'Lieutenant Crane spotted the van on Hollywood and Orange just a minute or two ago. It's heading away from the parking structure, but he decided to follow it anyway.'

'B.A. already picked them up, then,' Decker said. 'Tell

Crane to follow them from a distance and not to show himself! I want to be there when the lid comes down. . . !'

SIX

The klieg lights were cold and the bizarre premiere of 'Wine for Breakfast' had been consigned to history by the time two o'clock chimes rang somewhere down the Boulevard. The courtyard of the Chinese Theatre was vacant except for the lone figure of a self-made medium, who was huddled over the concrete slab containing hand and footprints left by John Wayne during the heyday of his film career. The gnarled woman, dressed in peasant garb with a woollen babushka tied tightly around her head, was muttering a cryptic incantation as she poured into the indentations a vile ochre concoction that would have turned a witch's stomach. When she had finished her chant, the woman reached for the candle that was providing her illumination and tilted it so that some of the wax dripped into the liquid pool, forming small islands. She next withdrew a stick of incense from somewhere in the folds of her dress and lit it, then slowly lowered the glowing, fragrant tip to the Duke's puddled footprints. One of the ingredients in the medium's brew was flammable, for suddenly the liquid was afire and giving off a thick, pungent cloud that varied in colour from green to blue. The woman stared wide-eyed at the rising smoke, nurtured by the hopes that it would soon take the form of the man whose immortal soles were craddling the liquid.

As the woman was raising her arms in supplication and calling the smoke by name, a taxi pulled up to the corner and Daniel Running Bear stepped out, handing the driver a five dollar bill.

'Keep the change.'

'Hey, thanks, pal,' the driver said, pocketing the five.

'You know, Las Palmas is only a couple blocks down the Boulevard. I can give you a lift that far, no problem.'

'That's okay, I can use the walk.'

'Okay. Just keep your eyes peeled. 'bout this time the psychos start coming out of the woodwork.'

'I appreciate the warning.' Daniel stepped up to the kerb and waved a farewell to the cabbie, then started down the sidewalk. Out of the corner of his eye, he saw the dying cloud of smoke in the theatre courtyard and the woman kneeling before it. On a hunch, he went to investigate.

As the Indian entered the courtyard, he first appeared to the medium through the haze of smoke. Letting out a gasp of triumphant exultation, she rose to her feet and clutched her withered hands together.

'John, dearest John,' she muttered almost delirious with joy. 'You've come, come at last, my love. Now I can . . .' When Daniel came close enough that she could see his features, she suddenly recoiled in horror. 'No, you're not John Wayne! There's been a mistake! What have I done!'

Daniel smirked and shook his head. 'Come on, Hannibal . . . or is it Peck this time? The joke's over. Can we discuss – '

'You!' the medium hissed, taking another step away from Daniel. 'The bringer of death from *Stagecoach*! Away! Ach, the chant's gone awry!'

The woman crossed herself repeatedly and continued to retreat, accidentally kicking over her candle putting its dim light out.

'Look, enough is enough!' Daniel took a few long strides and caught up with the medium. He pulled off her babushka and began tugging at her hair, saying, 'Come on, take this wig off already!'

'Not my scalp!' the woman wailed, lashing out with her hands in sheer desperation. Her long nails on one hand stung the bruises on Daniel's face while her other fingers sharply jabbed his cast, forcing him to pull away from her in pain. The medium took advantage of Daniel's distraction to turn heel and take flight into the shadows, all the while mumbling a stream of curses intended to protect her from any further harassment at the hands of the conjured demon she had mistakenly summoned forth from the nether realm.

'Wait, Hannibal!' Daniel called out, reluctantly giving chase. 'Can't we quit playing games?'

Whether by invocation of another chant or mere sleight of foot, the woman was nowhere to be seen when Daniel emerged from the courtyard and checked up and down the Boulevard for a trace of her. He finally stuffed his hands into his pockets and walked the few blocks east to the corner of Las Palmas and Hollywood Boulevard. He failed to encounter the mystery woman, but several beggars accosted him from darkened doorways and a pair of slit-skirted prostitutes across the street called out to him, offering a special two-for-one offer, valid only for the next half-hour. He passed, and the women soon after flagged down a likely-looking mark cruising the boulevard in an Olds Cutlass.

When he reached the corner, Daniel took up a position beneath the streetsign and checked his watch. It was now almost ten after two. He looked around and saw a number of offbeat characters roaming the sidewalks, any one of which he figured could be a member of the A-Team. The vast majority of them, though, he realized were losers who only came out in force this late at night because it was the one time they could mingle without feeling out of place. He felt a slight aversion for them, but also a measure of sympathy. After all, he knew that, but for a string of favourable circumstances, he could be one of these doomed souls, trapped in a dark, ongoing present with little sense of past and no hope for the future.

As Daniel was glancing down one side of the street, a figure blindsided him from behind, although with only a meagre amount of force. Daniel quickly regained his balance and whirled around to find himself staring into a wasted, deep-furrowed face with eyes so bloodshot and disorientated that he doubted they could be part of a disguise. The man could have been anywhere between thirty and three hundred. He was missing half his teeth, he reeked of sweat and cheap wine, and his breath could repel insects and debutantes from thirty paces.

It was clear to Daniel that the man had blundered into him accidentally, because his next set of shuffling steps brought him careening off the brickwork of the nearest storefront and he almost crumpled to the sidewalk from the impact.

'Are you okay?' Daniel asked. 'What's wrong?'

'Nothin',' the man mumbled, catching himself before he fell and then using parking meters for support as he tried to drag himself along. 'Nothin' 'tall.'

Overcome by his humanitarian instincts, Daniel moved away from the signpost and tried to catch up with the other man. 'Hey, wait a minute . . . are you sure you couldn't use some help?'

The transient stopped and pivoted awkwardly, boring his bleary eyes into Daniel's. 'Kin help m'self . . . don't need no help. Never got it and ain't startin' now . . .'

'Hey, I just thought . . . maybe you could use some food?' Daniel reached to his rear pocket, and the other man suddenly picked up his speed, bounding off the sides of parked cars as he tried to stay on the kerb. Daniel soon realized why the transient was in such a hurry. 'My wallet!' he cried out, finding his rear pocket empty.

The wino's head start wasn't far enough for him to evade a quick apprehension. Daniel caught him halfway down the block and swung him around in a fit of temper, angry at both the transient and himself.

'Don't mess with me,' the wino warned Daniel as the Indian quickly frisked him and found the missing wallet.

'Hey, I would have given you a couple of bucks,' Daniel told him. 'You didn't have to pull that with me . . .'

'Help!' the wino called out hoarsely, drawing the attention of the nearby lowlife. As Daniel released the man and looked around, he saw drifters moving towards him from several directions, all of them looking more healthy and dangerous than the petty thief.

'I don't want any trouble,' Daniel called out, trying to sound calm.

'Too bad,' one of the vagrants bellowed, rolling up a tattered shirt sleeve, revealing tattoos of snakes and scorpions. He was toting a broken beer bottle with deep, jagged edges. He didn't look like he was on his way to drop it off at a recycling centre, either.

Just then a siren wailed into life and a police cruiser turned the corner, washing the sidewalk with a blinding searchlight. The beam might have been spray from an insecticide for the way it sent the street pests scuttling to the sanctuary of the nearest dark alley. Only the wino who'd picked Daniel's pocket remained in the open, and that was because Daniel held him in a vice-like grip that would have resulted in broken bones if he tried to bolt free. The cruiser double-parked next to the cars closest to Daniel and his captive, and a burly officer got out from behind the wheel.

'What's the trouble here?' he asked, eyeing both Daniel and the transient.

Daniel could feel his prisoner quaking with terror, and he let go of the man as he told the officer, 'Huh? Oh, nothing, officer . . . no trouble . . .'

'No trouble, huh? You expect me to believe that?' The officer had his nightstick out and was tapping it lightly against his open palm. 'Let's have some I.D., gents.'

As the transient began fumbling through his pockets for identification that wasn't there, Daniel handed the officer his wallet, explaining, 'Look, we just had a little misunderstanding here. No big thing. If you'll let us – '

'I make the decisions around here,' the officer informed him, gesturing to his cruiser. 'Why don't we take a ride and kick this around awhile, okay?'

'Do we have to do this?' Daniel protested. 'Look, there's – '

'Let's go,' the officer interrupted, pointing at the others with the tip of his nightstick. 'Both of you.'

Daniel reluctantly left the kerb and walked between the two parked cars leading to the police cruiser. As the officer was opening the back door for Daniel, the transient suddenly broke into a drunken run, vanishing noisily into the night.

'Hey!' Daniel cried out. 'What about him?'

'Get inside,' the officer told Daniel firmly. 'He won't get far.'

Daniel slipped into the back seat. The officer closed the door, then walked around and got back in behind the wheel. As he drove off, Daniel asked him, 'Why aren't you even looking to see where he's run off to? What's going on here?'

'You almost lost a lot more than your wallet back there,' the officer said, taking one hand off the steering wheel to open the Indian's wallet. 'Daniel Running Bear. What are you doing in Los Angeles, Daniel?'

'I'm here to meet some people,' Daniel answered vaguely, glancing out the window at the vacated streetsign where he'd been waiting before his run-in with the transient.

'The A-Team maybe?' The driver grinned into the rear-view mirror, seeing Daniel's surprised reaction. 'Daniel, I'm Hannibal Smith . . .'

SEVEN

F. Scott Fitzgerald once remarked that being awake at three a.m. gave one the most accurate perspective of his lot in the universe, or words to that effect. It was an enchanted hour, seemingly divorced from the rest of time, when one's mind took on a life all its own and could exalt in grand schemes or wallow in that dark night of the soul that is the province of manic depressives and existentialists long overdue for a good time. Pity the poor fool who commits his thoughts of this time to paper and dispatches them through the mail in a fit of passion without waiting for the sobering rays of dawn to place them in more objective light.

Three a.m. was Howling Mad Murdock's favourite time, bar none. It was a time when the entire Veteran's hospital seemed lost in slumber, even the caterwauling souls in the rooms with rubber walls. It was a time so silent that one could hear water gurgling through pipes in the floor, beams creaking under the strain of tossing bedmates, and hot winds jostling the palm fronds on the grounds outside. It was a time when the distinction between nurse and patient was inconsequential, when there was no thought too outrageous to bear the ring of truth, and no one to say which thoughts were sane and which were mad. More important than all these factors, though, three a.m. was also when the local cable station broadcast reruns of 'Range Rider'.

Murdock sat transfixed on his bed as the appointed hour arrived, a plastic cap pistol in either hand and his face covered by the cardboard likeness of his favourite hero, cut years ago from the back of a cereal box that had long since lost the scent of corn flakes and was now taped in spots where time had taken its toll on Range Rider's dimpled chin and creaseless brow. There were holes in the mask's eyes, and Murdock was able to peer out at the flicker of black-and-white flashing across his television screen, recounting an adventure he'd seen so many times in his youth that he was able to mouth the dialogue simultaneously with the actors. Range Rider, astride a magnificent palomino, was rounding up a band of black-garbed desperadoes, firing twin six-shooters that seemed to spew more lead than gatling-guns, making the villains dance in the dirt with their hands raised as they begged for mercy. Murdock bobbed on his bed, going through the motions of a horseman in the saddle as he shot off caps and filled the room with smoke and sulphur. When an onscreen posse arrived to take the hombres into custody, Murdock mimicked Range Rider as the cowboy twirled his pistols and slammed them neatly into his holster before giving his trusty steed a swat on the hindquarters and riding off in search of the nearest sunset.

'And so,' Murdock announced along with the show's baritone narrator, 'the Range Rider defeats the Black Rock gang in another daring shootout, once again making the plains safe for all who dare brave the untamed west, no matter race or creed . . . the Range Rider stands for truth and justice for all!'

Elevated to heights of euphoria, Murdock reached for the remote control in order to flick off the television set before a used car commercial could intrude upon his fantasy. Before he could work the controls, however, the set blacked out of its own accord. The luminous hands on the clock next to Murdock's bed went dark as well, leaving him in a blackness that was only slightly alleviated by moonlight spilling in through the window across the room. Murdock welcomed the power outage, as it enabled him to stay in character with even more ease. Rocking gently on his mattress, he whinnied on behalf of his would-be horse, then began improvising a sequel to the episode he'd just seen.

'It's all right, girl,' he whispered, stroking the pillow that served as a horsehead. 'The Black Rock gang must have lured us into this cave and pushed a boulder across the opening. There has to be another way out.'

'How about right here, through the window?' a voice called out from the darkness.

'Who goes there?' Murdock demanded, raising his cap guns to defend himself.

'Put 'em away, would you, Murdock? It's me, Face,' Templeton Peck clambered through the window into the room, still wearing his tuxedo. He was carrying a flashlight and he shone the beam at Murdock's bed, revealing the Range Rider impersonator.

'Hey, Face, lucky thing you showed up with that flashlight,' Murdock said, quickly regaining his composure. 'There's some kind of blackout in the building.'

'That's because B.A. is jumping the master circuit so the alarms didn't go off when I opened the window.' Face brought the light up, spotting Murdock's mask for the first time. 'Hey, what are you wearing, anyway?'

Murdock whipped off his mask and hid it behind his back. 'I guess my secret is out,' he sighed with resignation. 'You have discovered my alter ego . . .'

'Come off it, Murdock,' Peck groaned, 'You're not Professor Nutty-Buddy again, are you? Or Rex the Wonder Dog?'

'No, no, no,' Murdock snapped indignantly. He put the mask back on, letting Face have a good look. 'When you called before you said we were going up against horse rustlers . . . and who better to defeat them than the masked lawman of the plains . . . the Range Rider!'

'You've got me there,' Peck conceded. As Murdock got up and threw a few items of clothing into a tote bag, Face started fluffing pillows and setting them beneath the blankets in such a way as to suggest the prone form of a dozing patient. For effect, he dangled a spare pair of sneakers out from the bottom of the sheets and exposed the brim of one of Murdock's baseball caps at the top. Heading back towards the window, he told Murdock,

'Come on. I told B.A. to give me ten minutes before he turns the juice back on. If the lights are out any longer than that they'll start a room check.'

'Right behind you,' Murdock said, lingering a moment at the headboard of his bed and pantomiming the untying of a slip knot as he whispered, 'Come, Thunder . . . good girl.'

'Aw, no . . .' Face paused halfway out the window and shook his head with disbelief at Murdock. 'Thunder's not what I think she is, is she . . . I hope.'

Murdock neighed quietly, then lightly caressed the air next to him as if soothing a troubled mare. 'Whoah, girl. Whoah, easy . . . we're just going to take a little trip. Remember how much you like Arizona? The Painted Desert – '

'Murdock, I don't know about this,' Face interrupted. 'You know how B.A. feels about Billy being in his van and he's just a dog. I think a horse is going to pose some definite problems.'

Murdock straightened, jutting his chin out as he proudly declared, 'The Range Rider would sooner face a dozen bandits without his six shooters than not have Thunder at his side. There isn't a man who stands tall enough to get between me and my trusty steed.' His position stated, Murdock began leading his faithful figment across the room. 'Come, girl.'

Face rolled his eyes and dropped from the window to the ground outside, then moved to one side to make room for Murdock. As Murdock was awkwardly making his escape, compensating for the bulky form of unseen Thunder, B.A. Baracus stole furtively along the outside wall to Peck's side, the gold chains around his neck clattering with each movement.

'Hey, man, what's the holdup?' B.A. demanded. 'We gotta scram! I shoulda had the lights back on already!'

'Well, B.A., you know how it is with Murdock.'

'What's that crazy fool up to this time?'

'You'll find out soon enough.'

Murdock reached the ground, landing a few feet from

B.A. but keeping his eyes on the window and making strange gestures with his arms. 'Atta girl, you can do it! Just like that time we broke out of the freighter when we were fighting the Pecos brothers!'

When Murdock had helped Thunder down to his satisfaction, he turned and found himself staring into the fierce dark eyes of his long-time foil, who blocked the way with his incredible bulk. Murdock propped his mask on his forehead and smiled.

'You better not be talkin' to no invisible animal, sucker!' B.A. warned.

'Who, me?' Murdock chuckled frailly.

'Man, why Hannibal thinks we need a nutbar like you helpin' us out is beyond me.'

'Far from a nutbar, I am merely feigning an alias,' Murdock sniffed. 'Once I don my mask, I become the true defender of – '

'I don't want to hear your crazy jive, Murdock!' B.A. retorted, starting off the way he'd come. 'Let's get outta here before we get found out and you end up back in your hatch!'

Face reached up and closed the window to Murdock's room, then bounded after his associates, sighing under his breath, 'Here we go again . . .'

EIGHT

Following Colonel Decker's orders, Lieutenant Crane had made sure he trailed B.A.'s customized black van from a distance that reduced the chances of arousing suspicion and triggering a chase that might have resulted in the A-Team once again avoiding capture. However, there was a price to be paid for such precaution. As Crane and his fellow officers had followed the van from a position several carlengths back in the late-night traffic, there were several occasions when changing signal lights along both Hollywood and Sunset Boulevards threatened to terminate the pursuit. In each instance, Crane had been forced to veer into the oncoming lane and race through the intersection, narrowly averting head-on collisions in the process. By the time the two vehicles had entered West LA, the van was more than a block ahead of the military sedan. Fortunately for Crane, though, B.A.'s destination was close at hand, and the van had rolled into the Veteran's Administration parking lot closest to the hospital building.

'What are they doing here?' Crane wondered as he made up the lost distance and pulled into the complex.

Corporal Louie Willippe, a sandy-haired man riding next to Crane, spoke out, 'I remember reading in the files on the A-Team about some guy named Murdock who's in the nut bin here. He served with them in Nam. Flyer of some sort.'

'Very good, corporal,' Crane commended Louie as he searched the parking lot for the van. Spotting it at the far end of the lot, half-hidden behind a supply truck, he circled around, parking the car a few dozen yards away in a spot that put the truck between them and the van. Killing the engine, he told the corporal, 'Now let's see if we can't arrange for the rest of the Team to wind up in confinement.'

Drawing their weapons, the two men slipped out of their car and stealthily crossed the parking lot to the supply truck, where they broke off in separate directions. Crane moved around the front of the truck; Louie took the rear. Once both men were positioned where they could view the van, Crane gave a slight hand gesture and they broke from cover, converging on the van from both sides, fingers on the triggers of their guns. They didn't need to use them, though, because there was no one in the van.

'Damn!' Crane cursed, peering in through the front windshield.

Louie came up next to him. 'I doubt that they've given us the slip, lieutenant. My guess is they're trying to spring Murdock. They'll be back.'

'I hope so.' Crane paused a moment, deliberating his next move. Finally he continued, 'I'm going in to check on things. There's a surveillance kit back in the car. I want you to slap a bug on this van. If it turns out that the whole Team doesn't show up to drive off, I want to be able to track 'em to their hideout.'

'Are you sure, lieutenant?' Louie questioned. 'I think we got a clear case of a bird in the hand if we just wait here and nab whoever shows up.'

Crane shook his head. 'Decker wants 'em all, package deal. I don't want to have to answer to him if we turn up short-handed and scare the others off. We're too close to a clean sweep. Now get to work on that bug. Of course, if they come up on you by surprise before you're finished, do what you have to.'

'Yes, sir.'

'And while you're back at the car, put a call through to Decker and tell him what's happening. He said he wants to be here, so tell him to hurry.'

Louie nodded and headed back across the parking lot

while Crane started up the walk leading to the hospital lobby. The main entrance was locked, but there was an orderly at the information desk, using the phone to talk with his girlfriend on company time. When Crane tapped on the door and stood under the porch light so that he was clearly visible in his uniform, the orderly cut short his call and came over to let the lieutenant in.

'Kinda late for visiting hours, lieutenant,' he told Crane, opening the door.

'This is business,' Crane said. 'Has anyone been by here the past few minutes that shouldn't be?'

'Can't say there has,' the orderly drawled.

'There's some men we think might be dropping in on a patient by the name of Murdock. They just pulled in – ' Crane stopped talking as the lobby was suddenly swept into darkness. He looked down the nearest hall and saw that the lights were out there as well.

'Hmmmm, that's weird,' the orderly mumbled.

'It's them!' Crane exclaimed. 'They're up to something! Come on, take me to Murdock's room!'

'In the dark? Lieutenant, it's way over on the east wing! Let's just wait a second; I'm sure the lights'll come on soon enough!'

'Don't count on it,' Crane said, waving his gun in the darkness. 'These guys are no slouches. Look, there's enough moonlight to give us an idea where we're going. Let's hit it.'

'You're the boss,' the orderly droned, starting down the hallway, walking slowly and holding his hands out before him to check for obstacles in the way. 'I tell ya, I'll be glad when they get this Murdock outta here. He's a real problem case.'

'How do you mean?'

'Aside from having a few screws loose, he's always in and out of here. Sometimes he just runs away for a few days. Other times he comes down with oddball ailments and has to be shipped out to special clinics. He costs us more paperwork than a whole ward of psychos.'

'That's very interesting,' Crane said. 'Just what is he in here for?'

'He's a schizoid. Must have a dozen different personas, all of 'em outta touch with reality. He keeps the doctors busy. They treat him kinda like a mascot.'

'Wonderful,' Crane smirked. 'I can hardly wait to meet him.'

The two men reached the end of one hallway and were halfway down another when the lights suddenly flickered back into life. The corridors became filled with activity as other orderlies and aides went to check on their patients in the wake of the blackout. When they reached Murdock's room, Crane peered in through the small portal in the door, seeing the makeshift dummy supposedly dozing on the bed, bathed in the glow of the television.

'Looks peaceful enough to me,' the orderly said, looking in over Crane's shoulder. 'You want I should go in and check?'

Crane shook his head. 'No, maybe the others haven't shown up yet.' Spotting a security guard striding down the hall, the lieutenant signalled him over and quickly ran down the situation, then asked the guard to have a few of his men scour the grounds and have someone keep an eye on Murdock's room to see if any members of the A-Team might try to gain entry. Satisfied that things were under control, Crane left the ward and departed through a side exit leading to the grounds. On a hunch, he backtracked along the base of the building, counting off windows until he was just outside Murdock's room. Crouching over, he inspected the ground and confirmed his suspicions, seeing a series of fresh footprints pressed into the soil. With some effort, he lifted himself up and looked into the room. From this perspective, he could clearly see that it was pillows rather than Murdock beneath the covers.

'I should have known!' the lieutenant sputtered, kicking at the dirt and picking up his stride as he hurried to the parking lot. He reached the sedan just as Decker was getting out of his crumpled vehicle next to it.

'What's happening, lieutenant?' Decker asked.

Crane pointed over the hood of his car at the half-concealed van, whose tail-lights were just flashing on as a puff of smoke shot from its exhaust. 'We might have hit the jackpot, Colonel.'

Inside the sedan, Louie rolled down his window and told the officers, 'I counted three men getting into the van. Full house. We should take 'em, right?'

'Wrong,' Crane said, pressing a hand on Decker's shoulder and guiding the colonel down to a squat as he bent over to get out of the view of the van, which was backing out of its parking space.

'What do you mean, Crane?' Decker hissed. 'Three men are all we're looking for. Smith, Peck and Baracus.'

'Four,' Crane corrected. 'One of those three is Murdock. My guess is we're still without Hannibal Smith.'

'Damn,' Decker muttered. 'Where's he?'

'I think we'll find out soon enough,' Crane said. 'Corporal, did you bug the van?'

'Yep,' Louie said, checking a transmission screen rigged under the sedan dashboard. 'I'm reading them loud and clear.'

As the van pulled away, the transmitter gave off a series of electronic bleeps, which were translated into directional readouts. Without seeing the van, Louie was able to tell which way it was going, how fast it was travelling, and how much weight it was carrying. Decker watched the A-Team race off, fighting back his urge to take up an immediate pursuit.

'Can you pick up what they're saying?' he asked Louie.

The corporal shook his head. 'Didn't have that kind of bug in the kit. Seems to me we've got enough to keep an ear on them, though. They can't go anywhere, drop anyone off or pick anyone up without us knowing about it.'

'If that's the case,' Decker said, 'we should have them all where we want them soon enough. I can't wait to put them out of commission once and for all . . .'

NINE

Foghorns moaned forlornly in the harbour at San Pedro, and the thick haze muted the rays of the dawn sun, keeping the docks cloaked in drab, weather-worn colours. There were some ships moored at the docks, preyed upon by sweating longshoremen who scuttled about like small insects, transferring cargo from ship to shore or vice versa. There were sections of wharf, however, where there was little activity and the boarded-up warehouses looked as if it had been years since they had known the bustle of healthy mercantilism. It was one of these warehouses, a dilapidated structure of corrugated steel and half-rotted wood, that B.A. Baracus drove his van to shortly after six a.m. Stopping before the main doors of the building's loading area, B.A. punched his horn twice and waited.

A pair of seagulls screamed as they coasted on an air current overhead, seemingly suspended in place. The tamed surf lapped through the pilings that supported the pier, sending wisps of spray drifting onto the docks. But there was no sign of motion within the warehouse.

'Maybe he didn't hear you over the waves,' Peck told B.A. as he stared at the door, riding in the front seat across from Baracus.

'Can't keep honkin' or somebody's gonna come to check things out,' B.A. said, shifting the van into neutral. He was about to get out to investigate when the warehouse doors suddenly creaked open. Hannibal nodded to B.A. and held the doors open until the van pulled into the deserted interior of the building.

'Anyone try to follow you?' Hannibal asked.

B.A. shook his head as he climbed down from the van. 'I was real careful.'

'I don't know, though, Hannibal,' Face confessed. 'It seemed almost too easy. We sprung Murdock without a hitch, even though I could have sworn there was a tail on us on our way to the hospital.'

'That was just some drunk, man,' B.A. told Face.

There was a rustling in the corner of the storage room, and Daniel Running Bear stepped forward cautiously, accompanied by a woman in her late twenties with dark hair and sparkling eyes.

'Miss Allen was good enough to get us down here,' Hannibal said, grinning at the woman. 'And we didn't have too many complications either, did we, Amy?'

'Very funny, Hannibal,' Amy said drolly, explaining to Face and B.A., 'I had to twist the staff photographer's arm to drive us down. You know Joe . . . he's the one that's fresher than any fish they haul in here. Having to owe him a favour is enough to make me ill.'

'Now, Amy, I'm sure once he gets some good shots of the grunions he'll call it square with you,' Hannibal said.

'Not likely.'

'Well, anyway,' Hannibal went on, launching into introductions, 'Face, B.A., this is our new client, Daniel Running Bear. Daniel, meet my associates, Bosco Baracus and Templeton Peck.'

'And I thought my name was out of the ordinary,' Daniel chuckled, swapping handshakes with the other two members of the A-Team.

'By the way, guys,' Hannibal said, 'where is Murdock?'

'He dozed all the way down here,' Face said. 'I think he needs his sleep.'

'That fool needs more than sleep,' B.A. complained. 'Hannibal, he thinks he's some jive cowboy star with a horse name Lightning.'

'Thunder,' Face said. 'The horse's name is Thunder.'

'There ain't no horse!' B.A. roared.

Hannibal glanced over at Daniel. 'You'll get used to them in time. We all like to cultivate our, shall we say, eccentricities? It helps to be unpredictable when you're in our line of work. Gives us an edge.'

As if to demonstrate the latest innovation in the Team's arsenal of eccentricity, Howling Mad Murdock emerged from the back of the van, his face obscured by the mask of Range Rider. Sauntering over to Daniel with a gait that would have made John Wayne proud, Murdock raised his palm like someone about to swear on a bible. 'How,' he greeted Daniel in Hollywood Apache. 'You must be Chief Running Bear who summon help to save 'em wild horses from being slaughtered by rustlers.'

'It just keeps getting better,' Daniel said sarcastically, eyeing Hannibal. 'First I get the runaround by a fortune-cookie philosopher, then I pay two bucks for a soydog from a degenerate vendor, then I get picked up by you playing a cop on Hollywood Boulevard . . . and now the Range Rider shows up.'

'You've heard of the Range Rider?' Face asked, incredulous.

Murdock crossed his arms majestically. 'Being a full-blooded American Indian and living on the open range of Arizona where the Range Rider dispenses justice, naturally he would have heard of me.'

'I also used to catch the Saturday morning reruns when I was getting my degree in Berkeley,' Daniel said.

'Touché,' Face snickered.

'Now that we're all acquainted,' Hannibal said, 'how about if we get down to business?'

'Well, the one thing that comes to mind with me,' Amy began, 'is why doesn't the Bureau of Land Affairs step in and do something about this rustling? Don't the mustangs fall under their care?'

'I've tried that route, believe me,' Daniel said. 'It's a lost cause. Like any other branch of government, they've got too much to govern and too few people to do the work. There's thousands of wild horses scattered throughout the states. Our case is just another pin on a map in some bureaucrat's office.'

'Every one of those horses is protected by laws,'

Hannibal reminded Daniel. 'If they're being rustled and you've got proof, why don't you bypass the desk people and go to the authorities, make some arrests . . .'

'I only wish it was that simple,' Daniel said. 'But when someone like Bus Carter breaks the law, it's very hard to bring charges against him. Being a large land holder, and with his standing in the local Cattle Rancher's Association, he's a very influential man in the county.' Gesturing to his bruised face and the cast on his arm, he added, 'He also plays dirty . . . and for keeps. It's going to take people with a lot of nerve and backbone to stand up to him. That's why I've come to you. I can't do it alone.'

'I can understand that,' Murdock said. 'Even the Range Rider needs the help of his horse.'

'Shut up, Murdock!' B.A. snapped.

Daniel's upper arm was wrapped with an elastic bandage rather than a cast. Using one hand, he quickly unwrapped the bandage, revealing a thick stack of currency strapped in place around his bicep. 'Here,' he said, prying the money free and handing it to Face. 'I had it saved up for a master's degree, but I think this is more important right now.'

One of Peck's more notable quirks was his ability to flip through a wad of bills in any denomination and count the total take in a matter of seconds. He plied his trade on the money Daniel had given him, then eyed the Indian's cast as he said, 'To be honest with you, Daniel, I've had most of my wardrobe already made for the year and I don't have anything that would go with broken arms. Soooooo . . .' He handed the bills back to Daniel, 'I'll just return this and wish you best of luck elsewhere. You might try the Marines. I hear they've been looking for a few good men. If you're lucky, they might have found them . . .'

Daniel took the money reluctantly, unable to hide his disappointment. 'Okay, so I told Mister Lee I could front more cash than I actually have. I'm sorry.'

'No you're not,' Hannibal said, unravelling the cellophane from his first cigar of the morning.

'You're right,' Daniel admitted. 'But I had to meet you so I could convince you how important this is.'

'We've had that happen before, haven't we, Amy?' Hannibal said.

There was a look in Amy's eyes that suggested her rapport with Daniel since their initial meeting had grown beyond the bounds of journalistic curiosity. 'It doesn't hurt to hear someone's problem,' she said defensively, trying to hold back the rush of crimson coming to her cheeks.

'And we always wind up workin' for nothin',' B.A. groaned. 'Man, the smog don't bother me so much I wanna go try to save a bunch of horses.'

As Murdock shot B.A. a resentful glance, Daniel said, 'But these horses have lived there as long as my people. They're part of the land . . . a part of my tribe. Surely you can appreciate the importance of one's heritage and traditions, Mr Baracus. After all, isn't that hairstyle you're wearing based on an African tribal cut?'

B.A. instinctively ran his hand across the strip of thick hair running down the centre of his otherwise shaved scalp. 'Yeah!' he said, softening visibly to his prospective client. 'Hey, you're the first dude in a long time that hasn't tried to call this a damn Mohawk! How'd you know that?'

'It's not important now,' Daniel said. Addressing the entire group, he made a final appeal. 'I'll raise the money I promised you eventually. I'm a man of my word. All I ask is that you at least come with me to take a look at the situation. If that doesn't convince you, you can still keep this downpayment and I'll try something else. How about it?'

There was silence in the warehouse as the others looked to the A-Team's spokesman. Hannibal diligently wet his cigar, then lit it and blew a wide ring of smoke. He stared at it until it began to break up, then smiled at Daniel and said, 'I guess someone who's crazy enough to go after three jeeploads of armed rustlers single-handedly on horseback deserves some kind of special treatment.'

Gratitude washed away the disappointment from

Daniel's features, and Amy seemed equally pleased with the decision. The same couldn't be said for B.A., though. Turning his back to the others, he lapsed back into cynicism. 'We're workin' for nothin' again . . .'

Murdock was inspired by the prospects of the new assignment. Taking in a deep breath and expanding his chest, he provided his own narration for his dementedly envisioned part in the mission. 'Once again, the mysterious Rider of the Range sets out on another thrilling adventure with his trusty steed, Thunder . . .' When B.A. spun around and levelled a withering gaze at him, Murdock weakly added, '. . . who is remaining behind this one time.'

Peck took the money back from Daniel and slipped it into his pants pocket as he headed for the warehouse doors, calling out over his shoulder, 'Well, guys, no time like the present. Shall we saddle up?'

He'd only managed to open the doors a crack when the wharf outside exploded with the reverberations of gunfire. The woodwork of the door sprayed splinters at Face from the destructive force of the bullets crashing their way into the warehouse. He slammed the doors shut and dove to the dirt as a second barrage whistled past where he'd just been standing.

'I think somebody forgot to pay the rent here,' he said, crawling on all fours away from the doorway.

Hannibal set his cigar on the front bumper of the van, then hunched over and approached a nearby window, which was caked with grime but still clear enough to provide him with a view outside. It wasn't a pretty sight. A quick scan revealed no less than a dozen armed officers peering at the warehouse through the sights of their rifles as they crouched behind various forms of cover. Colonel Decker was there, and Hannibal recognized him from the night before.

'I thought you said you weren't followed here, B.A.'

TEN

After the initial burst of gunfire, there was a lull on the docks as Decker waited for some reaction from the A-Team. When the warehouse remained still, the colonel motioned for his men to draw closer to the building. As the orders were carried out, Lieutenant Crane moved over next to Decker and said, 'Maybe we got 'em with the first volley.'

'Not likely,' Decker said. 'How many times do you kill four flies with the first swat?'

'Good point,' Crane said. 'Plus there's more than four of them. Remember that photographer down on the beach said there's two more in there with them.'

'Collaborators. I don't know about the Indian, but I've seen that reporter's name in the files a few times. I'm not going to quit playing hardball on their account.' Decker was carrying a bullhorn, and once his men were repositioned, he raised it to his lips and boomed, 'All right. This is Colonel Decker of the US Army. We have you completely surrounded.'

Lowering the bullhorn a moment, Decker snapped his fingers. Each of the armed officers raised their weapons in the air and fired off a single shot, demonstrating that he wasn't bluffing.

Inside the warehouse, the trapped party was lying low, save for Hannibal and Peck, who stayed near windows to keep an eye on things.

'This guy sure is more popular than Lynch,' Hannibal remarked, trying to stay calm. 'Look at the size of that fan club.'

'He doesn't sound very happy, either,' Peck commented.

'Maybe he went back and caught the premiere of "Wine for Breakfast",' Hannibal said. 'You know how nasty critics can be.'

'Why don't you save us all a lot of bother,' Decker shouted through the bullhorn. 'Give yourselves up . . . or I'll flush that whole building and everyone inside right into the sewer.'

Amy was huddled by the wheels of the van. 'Is this guy kidding?' she exclaimed, her voice cracking with uncertain fear.

'Sounds like he's crazy!' Murdock whispered.

'Maybe you oughta talk to him, then, sucker,' B.A. snarled.

'Maybe *I* should,' Daniel Running Bear suggested. 'After all, they probably haven't linked me with you yet. I could – '

Decker interrupted him with another threat over the bullhorn. 'You want me to start blasting, Smith? Those first shots were just hors d'oeuvres compared to what we've got stored up for you . . .'

Hannibal looked back at Daniel. 'I don't think this guy's open to plea bargaining at the moment.'

'We have to do something, Hannibal,' Face said. The others looked at Hannibal as well, and under the scrutiny of their collective gaze his composure began to ebb.

'I'm thinking!' he told them.

Another round of gunfire rammed into the building, knocking out several windows and putting more vents in the fragile walls.

'Think faster!' B.A. shouted at Hannibal.

Hannibal took a deep breath, then moved away from the window and approached the bullet-riddled doors. He opened them a sliver and called out, 'Hey, Decker, this is Smith. You ought to cool out a bit. What if we have innocent people in here with us?'

'Who might that be?' Decker retorted. 'Amy Allen? I'd hardly call her innocent.'

Amy cringed. 'So much for my virtue . . . if we get out of this, remind me to wring Joe's neck. It sounds like he's the one that tipped us off.'

'I don't know about that.' B.A. was also lying near the van, and from his position he was able to spot something stuck to the underside of the chassis. He pried it loose and swore, 'Damn, it's a bug!'

'Durndest insect I ever saw!' Murdock said.

B.A. hurled the device at Murdock.

Back at the door, Hannibal shouted, 'Okay, look – '

Decker cut him off with another blast through the bullhorn. 'No talk! You come out . . . or we come in. And you're not gonna like it if we come in . . . I'm giving you two minutes!'

Closing the door, Hannibal beamed with pride at his cohorts. 'What a negotiator! Two minutes. Don't you just love it? No matter how good they are, they always screw up somehow.' He moved over to the van, grabbing his cigar from the front bumper. 'C'mon, let's get the weapons out.'

'Two minutes?' Amy said dubiously, rising to her feet. 'What can we possibly do in two minutes?'

Hannibal opened the rear doors of the van and withdrew his favourite Browning automatic and a weathered makeup kit. 'You heard the man,' he told Amy cheerfully. 'We're going out the door.'

'Just like that? You mean we're surrendering? That doesn't sound like you, Hannibal.'

Hannibal grinned around his cigar. 'Who said anything about surrendering?'

'Oh oh,' B.A. mumbled as he came around to the back of the van. 'Hannibal's on the jazz . . . this is gonna be interesting . . .'

ELEVEN

'One minute and counting.' Lieutenant Crane glanced up from his watch and looked to the warehouse. The only activity was taking place around the building, where the Army sharpshooters were closing in, darting from cover to cover like bashful rodents sneaking up on fresh cheese.

'I wonder what they're up to,' Colonel Decker muttered to himself uneasily. 'I'm beginning to think we should have just burst in on them.'

'It's obvious they really have no choice,' Crane assured him. 'They can see we've got them. They'll surrender. It's cut and dry.'

'Maybe for anyone but Hannibal Smith,' Decker said. 'With him, nothing is cut and dry.'

'You sound like you know the man personally,' Crane rejoined. 'I thought the first time you ran into him was last night.'

'That's true,' Decker reflected, 'but I'm familiar with his breed. He and I have a lot in common besides rank.'

The lieutenant looked once again at the warehouse. No one appeared in the shot-out windows. The doors remained closed and there was no sound coming from within. The sense of desolation emanating from the rundown structure was almost overpowering, and Crane felt an inexplicable chill of uncertainty run down his spine like a finger dipped in ice. 'What can he do?' he said, the sudden nervousness lending a quaver to his voice.

This time Decker checked his watch. 'Well, we'll find out soon enough. By my count, they've only got thirty seconds before the fireworks start.'

Time seemed to plod and each second seemed

interminable. The marksmen ceased their jockeying for better positions and began concentrating on their aims, lining their sights on every conceivable opening through which the A-Team might either emerge or attempt to wage a desperate defence of the warehouse.

'Twelve seconds,' Crane began counting down. 'Eleven . . . ten . . . nine . . . eight . . . seven . . . six . . .'

'Wait a second!' Decker suddenly interrupted. 'Listen!'

From within the heart of the warehouse, a mechanical roar sounded like the roar of some great beast roused from slumber with an empty stomach.

'The van!' Crane cried out. 'They're going to try to make a run for it!'

Even as the lieutenant was shouting his warning, the doors of the warehouse ruptured outward and the black van charged out onto the pier with the ferocity of a bull set loose in the arena. A dozen rifles swung about and their owners pumped lead in a steady stream at the vehicle, which bore down on two MP sedans forming a barricade against the possibility of escape. The MPs had underestimated the power of the van's engine and the strength of its bumpers, though. The vehicle slammed squarely into the area where the two sedans touched, parting them enough to create a gap through which it could plough and continue rolling down the pier towards shore.

'The tyres!' Decker commanded, grabbing his pistol and drawing bead on the van. 'Aim for the tyres!'

There was a deafening chorus of gunfire as the marksmen fired at the van's Michelins. When several shots simultaneously ripped into the right front tyre, the van dipped sharply to one side as the wheel's rim rammed down hard on the planks of the pier. It was enough of a disruption for the van to pitch wildly out of control. Veering from the route to shore, the vehicle instead spun out, crashing through a stack of crates and barrels. The collision slowed down the van considerably, but not enough to prevent it from sliding past the uprights of the pier and over the side.

'My God, we got 'em!' Crane shouted, running alongside Decker towards the spot where they'd last seen the van. Behind them, the marksmen also began rushing over. By the time they worked their way past the splintered crates and barrels and peered into the waters of the harbour, a number of early morning fishermen and dockworkers had arrived on the scene as well. They all stared with wonder at the van, which was taking water in and sinking with slow certainty.

'Clear the way!' Decker shouted to the curiosity seekers gathered around the pier. 'C'mon, stay out of the way! This thing's not over yet!'

The colonel aimed his gun at the submerging vehicle, and most of the other officers did the same, waiting for the first sign of survivors trying to swim free of the van. Bubbles rose to the surface, but they were caused by air rushing out of the punctured sides and not exhaling escapees. As the crowd on the pier watched on, the van finally sank from view. Seconds passed, becoming minutes, and still no one broke the water's surface.

'Well, Colonel,' Crane said, breaking the tense silence on the docks. 'It looks like you stopped the A-Team once and for all.'

'Yeah,' Decker said. 'It looks that way.' He didn't say it with much conviction, though, and there was reason for his apprehension.

Back at the warehouse, Templeton Peck carefully inched open the back door, which faced away from the main causeway of the pier. He checked to make sure all of Decker's men had left the area, then eased the door open and signalled inside. One by one, Murdock, Daniel Running Bear, B.A., and Amy emerged from the warehouse, each of them carrying the more valuable supplies that had been stored inside the van. A few yards from the door, there was a staircase that led down to the shore and a clot of more deserted buildings that would provide adequate cover from the view of anyone who might venture back to the warehouse to see what the A-Team had left behind.

As the group headed down the steps, Amy whispered worriedly, 'What about Hannibal? Shouldn't we make sure – '

'He'll be okay,' B.A. told her. 'He's used to stunt work. He'll meet us where he said he would.'

'Are you sure?'

'Of course I'm sure!' B.A. said, anger masking his own concern. Before stepping down past the level of the pier, he looked past the warehouse at the crowd gathered across the way.

Amongst the fishermen still milling around the military police at the opposite end of the pier was a man in an oversized slicker and matching cap. As he nonchalantly broke away from the others and began trudging down the pier, he raised a cigar to his lips and puffed on it contentedly. Hannibal had bruised his thigh when he'd dived out of the van during its crashing through the crates and barrels, but other than that he felt fine, just fine . . .

TWELVE

At dawn the A-Team and their associates had been on the verge of an annihilation that might have made the Symbionese Liberation Army massacre of ten years before look like a popgun tournament. By midafternoon, however, they were cruising leisurely across the state line in Amy Allen's cramped convertible, basking in the smog-free radiance of Arizona border country. The transition had been every bit as dramatic as the overall change in circumstances.

The rendezvous point where Hannibal had linked back up with the others had been the public lockers located behind the bait-and-tackle shops adjacent to the docks. Hannibal had been forced to wait at the lockers for some time, since discretion had dictated that Peck and the others take a circuitous route that would limit the chances that they would be spotted carrying their cargo of custom tools, surveillance equipment, submachine guns, and other items that wouldn't fall under anyone's category of acceptable fishing gear. When the group had at last met, they'd used the lockers to relieve themselves of anything that didn't seem essential for their upcoming assignment. Everything else was secreted into war surplus tote bags purchased at a store down the docks, where gossip about the warehouse shootout and the sinking of the A-Team van was already well on its way to becoming part of San Pedro folklore. On their way to the bus terminal, the Team had narrowly avoided discovery when a pair of military police sedans leaving the docks had driven past them. Fortunately, the sedans had been driving in the middle lane, and a semi-truck to their right had obscured any possible view of the sidewalk for the officers. Reaching the terminal, a northbound bus whisked the group away from San Pedro and deposited them, a few hours later, at the downtown station, located a few blocks from Amy's apartment and her parked convertible. It was only after the car had been loaded up that Amy had bothered putting a quick call through to the Los Angeles Courier-Express, assuring her boss that, contrary to what he might have heard from San Pedro, she was alive and well and on her way to investigate a new story she didn't feel at liberty to discuss at the moment.

The major drawback to the Team's current mode of transportation was its size. Although commercials for the convertible had touted it as roomy enough for a family of six, even half-a-dozen Munchkins would have been elbowing each other's ribcages if they all tried to fit inside the car at once. And Munchkins the A-Team weren't. Although Hannibal, Amy, and Daniel Running Bear were almost comfortable in the front seat, the threesome in back were wedged together like salmon in a sardine can. B.A. was in the middle, and whenever he shifted in his seat, Murdock and Peck felt as if they were both going to squirt out onto the asphalt from the pressure. Peck tried to take his mind off his discomfort by concentrating on the scenery.

'Ah, beautiful, quiet, serene Arizona,' he said with only the barest hint of sarcasm. 'The comatose state.'

Out of consideration for the others, Hannibal's cigar was unlit. He took it from his mouth and looked back at Face, drawling, 'Maybe you should location scout your next movie here, eh, "boobie"?'

'No need to rub it in, Hannibal,' Face said. 'Now that I missed my own premiere, I'm sure I'm through as a producer. That career sure went fast. Talk about the sizzle and fizzle of Hollywood . . .'

'How about if you talk about nothin', sucker,' B.A. complained. 'It makes you breathe faster and I already got to put up with your lungs pushin' on my elbows whenever you inhale. Move over! Gimme more room!'

'Will you take it easy, B.A.,' Face pleaded. 'Look, if I

have to, I'll take the trunk instead of having you ground me into the ashtray. Okay?'

B.A. turned to his other side, where Murdock was zealously hoarding a few inches of unused space between himself and the armrest on the door. When B.A. tried to nudge him over, Murdock braced himself and resisted.

'Hannibal, this fool won't give me no room!' B.A. appealed.

'Hey, I didn't design this thing!' Murdock whined. 'There's just not room for the four of us back here.'

'Four!' B.A. retorted. 'What do you mean, four? There's three of us back here. Only three!'

'Well, now, B.A., I don't like to disagree, but – '

'Three, Murdock!' B.A. pried one of his arms free and grabbed his tormentor by the lapels of his jacket. 'Right?'

'I . . . I . . . I . . .' Murdock stammered.

'You hear me, sucker!?' B.A. roared. 'There's three of us. Ain't nobody else. No *body*, no *animal*. You got that? There's three of us!'

'Do us all a favour and say three, Murdock,' Face suggested. 'If you don't he's gonna bounce you down the divider and you'll be nothin' but a grease spot for the roadrunners to peck at.'

'Okay, okay, okay,' Murdock acquiesced. 'Three!'

'Very good,' Peck applauded. 'That wasn't so hard, was it?'

Murdock shook his head demurely, at the same time extending one arm out the side of the car so that he could hold onto his imaginary reins and let his trusty steed Thunder gallop alongside the convertible.

'Will you guys take it easy back there?' Amy shouted over the wind rushing past the windshield. 'On a reporter's salary I can't afford a new car every time you guys get together in it.'

'Now, Amy, it is a long drive and this isn't the most comfortable car,' Hannibal said. 'Admit it.'

'You guys are choosy beggars, that's all I have to say.'

Daniel shrugged, enjoying his proximity to Amy. 'I'm comfortable,' he declared with a smile.

B.A. was far from placated. 'Well, we wouldn't be

going through this if you hadn't ditched my van, Hannibal,' he said bitterly. 'You just said you were gonna lead those MPs off.'

'I did,' Hannibal replied calmly.

'But you didn't bring my van back, man! I worked hard on them wheels, and now they're bein' used for fish bait. It ain't right!'

'Hey, don't take it so hard, B.A.,' Hannibal told him.

B.A. sulked. 'It's gone, man. Ain't never gonna see it again.'

'Oh, I don't know about that,' Hannibal said. 'I'm sure it'll turn up, sooner or later . . .'

THIRTEEN

Even as Hannibal was speaking, a dock crane was pulling the A-Team van out of San Pedro Harbour for the benefit of Colonel Dexter and a sprinkling of onlookers who agreed that it was the biggest catch of the season in these waters. The driver's door was open from Hannibal's last-second escape, and as the vehicle was hoisted over to the pier, water gushed out of the opening and a few trapped fish swam through the spray to freedom.

'We aren't going to find anyone alive in that,' Lieutenant Crane reasoned.

'Dead or alive is my guess,' Decker murmured, stepping forward as the crane lowered the van to the planks.

'You think the bodies were washed out already?'

'Not really.' Decker spoke with a calmness that disturbed Crane.

'I don't understand, Colonel.'

'You'll see.'

Sure enough, when the two officers approached the van and peered in through the jarred door, they found only a few stranded fish slapping about in puddles on the floor and a few other items that had been knocked around by the various abuses heaped upon the vehicle over the past few hours.

'Empty,' Crane said, hardly able to believe it. He turned to Decker. 'We can drag the bay . . .'

'Don't waste the energy, Lieutenant.'

'Sir?'

'All the bodies couldn't have washed out,' Decker explained impatiently. 'Do I have to paint you a picture,

Crane? They gave us the slip again.' He took out his frustration on the van, kicking one of the good tyres like a moron at a used car lot. 'This is nothing but a red herring we all chased after while the A-Team made their break from the warehouse. I ought to have my head examined for letting them pull something like that on me. Damn it, I'm going to end up behind a desk next to Lynch if I don't wisen up!'

'It's not your fault, sir,' Crane ventured. 'I mean, if they had been in the van and we'd let them go, it would have been even more humiliating . . .'

'One man!' Decker railed, not about to be so easily appeased. 'One lousy man was all I needed to leave behind and we would have caught them trying to sneak out!'

As Decker slammed the van door and started away, pushing his way brusquely through the curiosity-seekers gathered around the pier, Crane followed half-a-step behind. Something was bothering him, and he finally put a finger on it. 'But, if they were all making their getaway from the warehouse, who was driving the van? Why didn't we at least get him?'

'Because it was probably Hannibal Smith, that's why.' Decker pointed to the rubble marking the path by which the van had taken its detour into the harbour. 'It would have been easy for him to duck out before the van went over, then drift off into the crowd before we caught up with him.'

As the two officers headed back toward the warehouse, Corporal Louie Willippe rolled down the window of Decker's sedan and poked his head out. 'Excuse me, Colonel, but I've got General Bullen on the horn. He wants an update on what's happening.'

'Tell him I'm indisposed,' Decker said.

'But what about the A-Team? He wants to know if they've been apprehended.'

Decker paused alongside the car, his mind racing for an alibi. Finally he yanked the door open and motioned for the corporal to get out, saying, 'Let me talk to him, alone.'

'Sure thing, sir.'

Once he was by himself in the sedan, Decker took a deep breath and picked up the carphone. 'Hello, General.'

'You got 'em?'

'Well, no, sir, not exactly.'

'What's that supposed to mean?'

'We took some people into custody, but it turned out they were imposters.'

'What?'

'Apparently the A-Team hired a group of look-alikes to come down to this warehouse, just to throw us off the scent. They even got some photographer for one of the local papers here to play along and tip us off about their would-be hideout. He thought it was just a prank . . .'

'Some prank! What you're telling me is you've failed.'

'Failed is a strong word, General.' Decker glanced out the window, making sure no one was listening to his embellishment. 'I mean, we did catch the people at the warehouse. They just weren't the right people. I plan to have them all interrogated so we can come up with some new leads and get back on the right track.'

'I tell you, Decker, I could have gotten this kind of results from Lynch . . .'

'Look, General, I'll give you Hannibal's head on a platter by the end of the week, with his sidekicks stuffed for appetizers. Count on it.'

'I am, Colonel. I am. I'll talk to you then.'

A dial tone buzzed in Decker's ear and he slammed the phone down in a fit of fury. 'Smug bastard!'

Lieutenant Crane had gone over to the warehouse to check with the investigative crew that had poured over the interior of the building for clues. When Decker caught up with him, he was conversing with an officer inside a truck equipped with state-of-the-art computers and other paraphernalia allowing them instant access to intelligence networks operating out of the Pentagon.

'What did you people come up with as far as prints go?' Decker asked. 'Any that don't match those of the A-Team or that reporter lady?'

The man in the truck handed a computer readout to Crane, who relayed the information to Decker. 'Daniel Running Bear. We had his prints on file through the military. He served from sixty-six to sixty-nine . . . light infantry in Nam. Also did some schooling up in – '

'Never mind that,' Decker snapped. 'Where's his current address?'

'He's a computer programmer in Arizona,' Crane read off the sheet. 'He still lives on the Chequea Indian Reservation where he was born.'

'How the hell did he fall in with the A-Team?' Decker wondered. 'This is a long way from the reservation.'

'Nam connection, maybe?' Crane suggested. 'He served earlier than most of the others, but there might be an overlap.'

'Well, it's all we have to go on so far.' Decker took the readout sheet from Crane and scanned it quickly before deciding, 'I think we should pay Mister Running Bear a visit . . . find out what his story is. I've got a hunch that's where our A-Team is headed . . .'

FOURTEEN

On Daniel's instructions, Amy turned off the highway and travelled down a few miles of two-lane blacktop that cut through the sparse grassland. A hearty wind was blowing hot air and raising small whirlwinds of dust like miniature tornadoes. Dislodged tumbleweeds lived up to their name by bounding playfully about the terrain until their progress was checked by the unmoving obstacle of an upright cactus or stoic oak. An occasional prairie dog or jackrabbit would engage in the strange ritual of bolting across the burning tarmac, usually just as the convertible was bearing down upon them. Amy spent a lot of time switching from the accelerator to the brake pedal trying to avoid flattening the small daredevils. The animals seemed unphased by the close calls, invariably missing their gory demises by mere inches and then pausing on the shoulder once they'd crossed the road to stare at the passengers in the car, who were looking back at them.

'I think they're laughing at us,' Peck said after the fifth time they'd braked for one of the animals.

'I say we knock it off with the stop and go!' B.A. complained to Amy. 'I'm tired of feelin' like I'm in a milkshake machine.'

'What do you want me to do, run them over?' Amy said testily.

'They're just playing games with us,' B.A. retorted. 'Damn little furballs are making us look like fools, man!'

Daniel intervened in the argument, saying, 'We're almost there. We won't have to put up with them much longer. I have to say, though, Amy . . . you can usually drive straight past them without putting on your brakes and they're still apt to get away from the tyres.'

'Are you sure?'

Daniel nodded. 'They have quick reflexes. Sometimes I think they do this just to stay in shape.'

'They sound like us,' Peck said. 'Never take the easy way . . .'

'I like that,' Hannibal reflected. 'I just love a good image.'

'You just love about everything,' B.A. sneered. 'Maybe you oughta sit back here and see if you just love bein' squeezed between the Face Man and this crazy fool Murdock!'

Hannibal smirked and confided to Daniel Running Bear, 'In case you hadn't guessed, B.A.'s nickname stands for Bad Attitude.'

Presently, billboards and a first sprinkling of homesteads marked the outskirts of Ohigai, a small town bordering the edge of the Chequea Indian Reservation. Not surprisingly, half the billboards touted the availability of Indian craftwork for sale at the eight different shops that comprised half of Ohigai's businesses.

'Many of our people hold to the old traditions,' Daniel explained. 'They do good work, then bring items into town here from the reservation for sale.'

As they headed into town, travelling down the main street, the A-Team glanced out at the various storefronts and the makeup of those roaming the sidewalks.

'Looks like all tourists to me,' Face said.

'That's pretty much what Ohigai's about,' Daniel said. 'Last census they figured out there were seventeen percent Native Americans working here. Most of my people prefer to stay at the reservation. You don't see them around here because they usually come into town early or late in the day, when they're less apt to have to put up with the camera crowd. Some tourists can be pretty insensitive . . . oh, Amy, you'll want to pull into those stables at the end of the street, okay?'

'Stables?' B.A. said. 'What are we goin' to some stables for?'

As Amy pulled into the lot next to the stables, which advertised rental horses, Daniel looked back at B.A. and grinned. 'You said you were tired of riding in the back of this convertible, right? Well, this is the easiest way to get where we're going, believe me.'

'Cowboys and Indians,' B.A. mumbled as the group piled out of the car. 'Man, this is crazy!'

Daniel went over to talk with the proprietor of the stables while the others went to inspect the horses corralled out back. Murdock rubbed his hands together excitedly and rushed forward, stroking the mane of a complacent Apaloosa as he gushed, 'Oh, man, horses! I love horses!' He looked over his shoulder at B.A. 'Don't you just love horses?'

'When I can see 'em!' B.A. taunted. 'When I can see 'em, I can stand 'em.'

'But can you ride 'em, that's the important question,' Face said.

'Do I getta choice?' B.A. said.

Hannibal came up next to Baracus and draped an arm over his shoulder. 'Look at it this way, B.A., at least we're not flying, right?'

B.A. didn't seem overly relieved by that pronouncement. Eyeing the horses on the other side of the fence they were gathered around, he said, 'All I can say is my kinda Mustang has four wheels and the horse is under the hood.'

Daniel rejoined the A-Team, introducing them to the owner of the stables, who happened to be his cousin. Once the formalities were dispensed with, the owner pointed out the best mounts available and had several of his assistants help suit them up for riding. Ten minutes later, Daniel and the A-Team were in the saddle and on their way up a winding horsetrail that led from the stables to the open expanse of the reservation. The path was wide enough for them to ride two abreast, and Daniel took the lead with Amy beside him, answering her barrage of questions about everything from the surrounding topography to his life story.

Hannibal and Peck were next in the caravan, and they glanced at one another after having viewed the interplay between those in front of them. 'What do you think, Face?' Hannibal asked Peck quietly. 'Is she just being a good reporter or do we have a romance blooming before our very eyes?'

Face thought it over. 'Well,' he finally observed, 'Cupid's known for his aim with a bow and arrow. This is definitely his kind of territory.'

B.A. was riding by himself behind Hannibal and Peck, refusing to team up with Murdock, who was glad to be bringing up the rear, as it gave him a chance to don his Range Rider mask and engage his delusions of grandeur with the least interruptions.

'Nice of you to meet me here, Thunder,' he whispered to his horse, now a true beast of flesh and blood. 'I knew I could count on you.' The horse responded to a light tug on its reins by neighing slightly and cantering forward, close to the hindquarters of B.A.'s steed.

'Hey, back off, sucker!' B.A. warned, flexing his biceps as he pointed an angry finger at Murdock.

Murdock eased off on the reins, falling back to his previous position as he soliloquized softly, 'At the request of the general himself, the Range Rider consents to protect the rear flank of the expedition as it makes its way through the treacherous, bandit-infested pass, ever on the alert – '

'What are you babblin' about, Murdock?' B.A. shouted over his shoulder.

Murdock sat upright in his saddle and pulled an imaginary zipper closed across his lips. When B.A. turned back to face the way before him, Murdock broke the seal and shot his tongue out at Baracus.

In little over an hour, the riders had traversed the lowlands and foothills leading to the rolling, rock-encrusted terrain where Daniel had thwarted Bus Carter's men and almost lost his life for his trouble. As they stopped along a ridgetop overlooking a long, grassy vale, Daniel motioned down the incline and said, 'There they are . . .'

Wild mustangs were frolicking rambunctiously through the grass below, their manes flowing gracefully as their sinuous limbs carried them along with powerful ease. Their every motion spoke of unbridled majesty, of a carefree ebullience that Daniel and the others could only admire and envy. Amy had brought along a camera and tripod stand, and she dismounted with Daniel's help to set up for some shots of the stallions and wild mares.

'Daniel, they're gorgeous!' she said as she readied the camera.

Daniel nodded, sadness in his features. 'There's fewer of them from when I was last here. Carter's men probably made another raid on them already and rounded some up.'

'Where's the border between your land and Carter's?' Hannibal asked Daniel.

'Actually,' Daniel said, 'this is all reservation land, but when the government gave it back to the Indians, they made a provision that it all be designated open grazing. We had no objection to that at all, but Carter had problems with the ruling.'

'How so?' Face asked.

'As near as I can figure, he feels that since his cattle has already been grazing these hillsides for a decade, they have more rights to the land than the horses.'

'I don't follow you, Daniel,' Hannibal interrupted. 'I mean, there's a lot of grass around here. Why can't everybody just share?'

'It doesn't work that simple, I'm afraid.' Daniel pointed to the frenzied activity of the mustangs and said, 'With the way the horses have been multiplying over the years, it's gotten to the point where they can wipe out a whole hillside in a matter of days. It would take grazing cattle at least a month to do the same job, and there's more of them than there are of the horses. We've tried several times to meet with Carter to work out some solution to his problem, but he won't pay any attention to us. Instead, he just sends his men out to get rid of the horses when he thinks no one's looking.'

'Which takes care of his cattle and his pockets,' Amy said contemptuously as she peered through her viewfinder and focused on the mustangs before taking a series of shots with her telephoto lens. 'It's obscene to think that anyone could see these horses and want to deprive them of their freedom.'

Daniel smirked bitterly. 'I think they do more than deprive them of their freedom.' As Amy was struggling with the import of the Indian's words, Daniel told Hannibal, 'My nephew was out here one night a couple of weeks ago and saw Carter's men rounding up horses for the first time. Until then, we'd only had suspicions.'

'And where does Carter take them once they're rounded up?' Hannibal asked.

'At first? I have no idea, really. The man owns over two hundred and fifty thousand acres around here.'

Hannibal whistled low. 'That's a lot of land, my friend. Wherever he puts 'em, though, I'm sure he doesn't sit on 'em too long. You said something back in LA about him getting them out by rail . . .'

Daniel nodded. 'That railroad track we passed on our way out of the stables is his own private line. He has a locomotive and boxcars he uses to run his cattle out. I'm sure he takes the horses down to a slaughter-house in Mexico. The state line's only a few miles from here.'

'Oh, my God . . .' Amy gasped. 'He kills the horses!!?'

'I think it's a safe bet.'

Amy looked at Hannibal. 'We have to do something! There's no way we can turn our backs on this now!'

Hannibal watched the horses prance through the valley a few moments more, then he looked over at Daniel and said, 'Amy's right. You've got yourself the A-Team . . .'

FIFTEEN

Amy wanted to get some closer photos of the mustangs, so Daniel led the party down the ridge to the valley, taking a course that wound through the thickest concentration of cottonwoods and rock outcroppings to minimize their chances of alarming the horses.

'I just wish I had a video camera,' Amy said, watching the mustangs as she rode. 'A few minutes of footage on the evening news would probably make more of an impact than any story I'm going to be able to come up with.'

'You'll be surprised how much you can capture with a still camera,' Daniel told her. 'I once brought a sculptor up here to take some pictures as inspiration for a piece he was working on, and he got some incredible shots.'

'Yeah, well, we were in such a rush to leave my apartment back in LA that I brought my old camera instead of my new one. I'll be lucky if the exposures turn out right.'

'If they don't, I have a good camera at my place,' Daniel told her. 'I could take you back here another time.'

'I'd like that,' Amy said with a smile. 'Thanks, Daniel.'

'You can call me Dan.'

The group was travelling at closer ranks than previously, and B.A. nudged his horse forward, coming up on Daniel's left side and putting an end, for the time being, to Amy's budding romance.

'What about your people, man?' B.A. asked Daniel. 'How can they let Carter get away with this? Seems to me they'd just gang up on the dude and teach him a thing or two . . .'

'Hardly,' Daniel said. 'They're just people like anybody

else. They live their lives and go about their business like anyone would in any community. Since this doesn't directly affect most of them, they figure they've got better things to do with their time. They're not going to dig out the old war paint, saddle up and ride on Bus Carter's hacienda. A hundred years ago, they might have thought about it, but even then I doubt that they would have resorted to any strong retaliation. It's not the Chequea style. Never has been.'

'I don't get it,' B.A. murmured.

'It's simple, B.A.,' Murdock piped in, spouting off like an Indian scout at a debriefing. 'The Chequeas were never a warring tribe. They were fishermen who migrated south during the war in eighteen sixty-four.'

'No kidding?' Face said, overhearing Murdock.

'He's right,' Daniel confirmed.

'How'd you know that, sucker?' B.A. asked Murdock.

'It's the Range Rider's business to know such things,' Murdock sniffed haughtily.

Hannibal withdrew his unlit cigar and chuckled, 'B.A., I think what Murdock's trying to say is he got the info off a cereal box when he was knee-high to a grasshopper . . .'

'Same place he got his face, right?' B.A. said, glancing at the mask propped up on Murdock's forehead.

Leading the group around one last bend leading to the valley floor, Daniel said, 'My ancestors lived off the Colorado River and its tributaries. Like Mr Murdock says, they were particularly good at fishing and managed – '

Daniel's lecture was interrupted by a dissenting vote from an unseen spectator, who fired an arrow down at them from the cover of a rock cluster a few dozen yards uphill. The pointed shaft whistled past B.A. and was slowed down as it ripped into the leather of Peck's jacket.

'Get down, everyone!' Daniel shouted, leaping from his horse and dragging Amy down from hers, protecting her with his body as they dropped to the dirt. B.A. and Murdock dismounted with cat-like agility, cushioning their falls and springing back to their feet as they immediately set out in the direction the arrow had come from. Peck and Hannibal were leaning low astride their horses, trying to decide if they should stay in the saddle to take up the chase. The unseen attacker helped make up their minds by firing another arrow, which missed Hannibal by scant inches before imbedding itself in the trunk of a tree next to him. Both men quickly slid to the ground and slapped their steeds' hindquarters to chase them out of the line of fire. Hannibal looked up at the rock cluster and caught a brief glimpse of a figure retreating from the edge of the outcropping.

'He's making a run your way, B.A!' Hannibal cried out.

As B.A. kept his eyes open for the would-be assailant, Hannibal scrambled to give assistance and Murdock broke off in the other direction to guard against the possibility that whoever had shot at them might change his course. Back down on the valley floor, Face secured himself behind a boulder next to Daniel and Amy, then pulled the arrow free from his jacket.

'Heck of a way to fish,' he said.

'Let me see that.'

'Be my guest,' Face told Daniel as he gave him the projectile. 'Any more come by, you can have those, too.'

Once Daniel had inspected the arrow, he clucked his tongue and rose from his crouch, muttering to himself as he started up the slope. Peck went over and helped Amy to her feet. She was wincing as she rubbed her side, but she told Peck, 'Don't worry about me. I'll be fine. Let's go see what's happening.'

Hannibal, Murdock, and B.A. were already halfway up the slope, waging a three-pronged pursuit of the archer, who paused now and then to give away his position by firing another arrow to slow down the A-Team. Most of his shots were at Murdock and Hannibal, though, and B.A. was able to gain ground until he'd managed to reach the edge of an escarpment that the sniper was unloosing his last arrow from. When the archer lowered his bow and leapt from the rocks, hoping to land on the run and continue his escape, B.A. was waiting for him and managed to get his fingers on the fleeing figure's leg, felling him. There was a brief scuffle as B.A. found himself trying to get a better grip on a human dynamo, but finally he pinned the archer down and realized that he'd apprehended a youth who looked at least a few months shy of his teens.

'You're just a kid!' B.A. said. 'What's the story, junior? You tryin' to hurt somebody for kicks or what?'

The youth turned his head away from B.A. and refused to talk. Before B.A. could try a more persuasive means of starting up a conversation, Daniel arrived on the scene.

'Hey! Hey, wait, B.A!' he shouted, rushing to where the youth was struggling anew against B.A.'s unbreakable grip. 'Don't hurt him. Shelly! Shelly, it's me!'

The boy looked over B.A.'s shoulder and spotted the other Indian staring down at him. 'Dan! Dan . . . what the – '

'Watch your tongue, Shelly,' Daniel advised the youth, at the same time signalling to B.A. that it was all right to release him.

Once he was freed, Shelly rose to his feet and dusted himself off, telling Daniel, 'I thought you were still in Los Angeles . . .'

'I just came back this afternoon,' Daniel explained. When the rest of the group had reached the escarpment, he introduced them all to the youth. 'Everybody, this is my nephew, Shelly. He's the one I was telling you about earlier. He was the first to spot Carter's men rustling.'

Hannibal stepped forward, extending his hand. In it was one of the several arrows that Shelly had fired at him. 'Please to meet you, Shelly, and I believe this is yours . . .'

B.A. was still worked up. Confronting Shelly, he demanded, 'What're you, crazy, firing those things at people? You could hurt someone bad if you hit them with one of those.'

Poking a finger into the hole in his jacket, Face wisecracked, 'They're not exactly great on leather, either.'

'I don't hit anything unless I want to,' Shelly boasted,

picking up the bow that had been dropped during his scuffle with B.A. 'I happen to be county champion. I was just trying to scare you off. I thought you were Bus Carter's men.'

'These people came back with me to help, Shelly,' Daniel told him. 'It took some doing to convince them, and you haven't helped ease their minds about their decision.'

'Yeah?' Shelly said brightly, showing no remorse for having come close to executing the A-Team. He asked them, 'You're gonna help us trash Carter and his men?'

'"Trash" Carter? Shelly and Dan Running Bear?' Face mumbled, shaking his head. 'I'd love to see how Sitting Bull would swallow all this.'

'Times change,' Daniel said. 'He'd probably want people to call him Joe . . .'

SIXTEEN

The setting sun was throwing long shadows across the flatlands by the time the A-Team and their Chequea consorts returned to the stables in Ohigai. Daniel settled accounts with his cousin while the others dismounted and massaged the sore backs and chaffed thighs they'd earned during their stints on horseback.

'Man, I've felt better after spending a whole day on a dirt bike,' B.A. said, twisting his muscular frame quickly back and forth to work out kinks. 'If we gotta play cowboy to wrap up this job, I think I'm gonna pass and head back – '

'Now, now, B.A.,' Murdock scoffed, strolling alongside Baracus as if he were feeling no pain. 'When you've been in the saddle as long as I have, you adjust to the rigours of riding. Me, I could go on for hours. Give it time, my friend – '

Murdock was about to pat B.A. good-naturedly on the back when the black man whirled around, throwing a half nelson on his gangly associate. 'I ain't in the mood for your babble, sucker, hear me?' he seethed, adding more pressure to Murdock's arm.

'Hey, lighten up, B.A.,' Hannibal said, coming over to mediate the altercation. 'And you, Murdock . . . ease off on the schtick, okay?'

'Yeah, Murdock,' B.A. said, releasing his grip on the other man. 'You wanna drive someone nutso, go talk to Tornado . . .'

'It's Thunder,' Face reminded B.A. 'His horse's name is Thunder. I already told you that, B.A., remember? Look, just think of the way pounding hooves sound in a cheap western. Hooves, thunder . . . it's easy.'

B.A. retorted, 'I don't care if its name is Partly Cloudy With Chance of Showers, I don't want nothin' to do with it!'

'All right, knock it off, all of you!' Hannibal shouted, waving his cigar like a penalty flag. Once the others had settled down, he shook his head and said, 'Why is it I always end up feeling like some vice-principal holding detention whenever I'm with you guys?'

'Probably because B.A. and Murdock never finished high school,' Peck said glibly.

Before the putdown could trigger a new squabble, Amy wandered over to the men and said, 'Look, guys, I'm going to take a ride out to the reservation with Daniel and Shelly. Here, you can use my convertible as long as you leave it in one piece . . .'

As Hannibal accepted Amy's keys, he looked past her at Daniel, who was starting up a dust-layered land rover parked next to the stables. Shelly was seated in back, bow across his knees, hands clasped around the roll bar.

'What's happening at the reservation?' Hannibal asked, keeping an innocent face. Amy saw through it, though, and her journalistic facade began to crumble. The smirks coming from Peck and B.A. didn't help matters, either.

'You know . . .' Amy said, struggling to prop up her supposed premise. 'I want to get some background information . . . talk to some of the elders, get their perspective on the problem. There could be a good human interest angle in all this . . .'

'I'm sure there could,' Face snickered.

Amy ignored the jibe. When Daniel drove over, she climbed into the land rover next to him.

'We'll find a place here to bunk down, then get our hands on a couple of things I think we might need,' Hannibal said, slipping Amy's keys in his pocket. 'We'll call you when we're ready to roll.'

'You've got the number I gave you earlier?' Daniel asked.

Hannibal nodded and waved as the Indian drove off down the main street of town.

Halfway down the block, two jeeps were parked in front of a feed store. Both vehicles belonged to Bus Carter and were only a few hours out of the repair shop after being mended of the damage inflicted during the encounter with Daniel Running Bear a few days before. Stryker and Dexter were loading sacks of feed into the older of the two jeeps. In the other, a young woman with the look of city breeding sat in the front seat, holding a vanity bag in her lap. The rest of her luggage was stacked behind her in the back seat and trunk. She yawned primly as she waited for the men.

'Almost through, Miss Carter,' Dexter wheezed, hefting one of the last sacks into the first jeep.

'We shouldn't be much longer at all, Lane,' Stryker added, shifting loads in the trunk to make sure they were secure. 'Hope you don't mind the delay. I know it was a long flight, but seein' how this is on the way back from the airport, we thought we'd kill two birds with one stone.'

'No problem,' Lane said. 'The whole purpose of this vacation is to relax and slow down my pace.'

'Your uncle is mighty anxious to see you, that's for certain,' Dexter said.

'I'm glad. I've missed him, too.'

With all the supplies loaded, Stryker signalled for the two men riding with Lane Carter to head out. The driver started his engine as Stryker did the same with the other jeep. Checking the street for traffic, the bristly foreman spotted Daniel approaching them in the land rover.

'Well, well, look who we have here . . .' Stryker quickly rammed his gears, shifting into reverse and backing up until he'd managed to block the road. The driver of the other jeep caught onto Stryker's game and hit the brakes, reinforcing the barricade. Lane frowned with confusion.

'I don't understand,' she told her driver. 'What's the matter?'

'Just a little unfinished business, ma'am,' he told her.

Daniel brought his land rover to a stop a few feet from Stryker's jeep. Shifting to neutral, he left the engine running and called out, 'Get out of my way, please.'

'"Please?"' Stryker snorted, baring an unhealthy grin. 'So you *did* learn a thing or two about how to act in front of people. Good, 'cause next time we have a little run-in – '

'There isn't going to be a next time,' Daniel countered firmly.

'You've got that straight,' Dexter put in.

Shelly stood up in the back of the rover and pointed a warning finger at Stryker and the others. 'You're not stealing any more of those horses! We won't let you!'

Lane flinched at the accusation and asked Stryker, 'What's he talking about?'

'Beats me, Lane,' Stryker said. 'Must be he's been eating them funny mushrooms and seein' things.'

Dexter shuffled a wad of tobacco from one cheek to another, spitting the leftover residue out the side of the jeep, just missing the front fender of the land rover. 'Kid back there's got a crazy mouth on him, Tonto,' he told Daniel. 'Maybe someone oughta teach him to respect his elders.'

'I can think of some other people who need the lessons more,' Daniel said coolly.

'Look,' Amy cut in, glaring at Dexter and Stryker, 'Don't you think you've done enough?'

'Hardly, ma'am,' Stryker said with mock politeness. 'We're only just starting.'

As Stryker and the others continued to bait the threesome in the land rover, Hannibal caught wind of the confrontation and stopped near the entrance of the hotel he was about to enter with his three cohorts. When they saw him looking down the block, the others diverted their gazes as well. Murdock was the first to react, reaching for his mask. 'Looks like a job for the Range Rider.'

B.A. made a move for Murdock, muttering, 'I'm gonna shut this crazy fool up for good . . .'

Hannibal stepped between the verbal sparring partners. 'Actually, this time Murdock happens to be right.'

'Wonders never cease,' Peck said. 'How's he right, Hannibal?'

By way of reply, Hannibal withdrew a bandana from his pants pocket and folded it diagonally before using it to mask the lower part of his face.

'Oh, I get it,' Peck said, following Hannibal's lead. 'What's this make us, Rangerettes?'

'I'll see that you're properly deputized when it's all over,' Murdock promised.

B.A. was the last to don a handkerchief, but it did little to disguise the prominent hair-style of his Mandinka. 'Let's go,' he shouted through the cloth.

'They'll never recognize us,' Face said, rolling his eyes at the sight of B.A.

By the time the A-Team had reached the three stalled vehicles in front of the feed store, a small crowd had gathered to watch Stryker's men jump down from the jeeps and fan out to surround the land rover on foot. They were so preoccupied with the threesome in the vehicle that they didn't notice that they had company until Hannibal called out, 'Looks like you guys are short a few partners for the square dance.'

Stryker looked over his shoulder and saw the A-Team approaching like cast members in a Ken Russell remake of *High Noon*. 'Who the hell are you?' he demanded.

'The fearless defender of the plains,' Murdock trumpeted in a voice intended to strike fear into the hearts of the rustlers. 'The Range Rider and his trusty companions!'

Instead of fear, Stryker's men reacted with amusement, snickering cockily at the mismatched group closing in on them. In the land rover, Daniel looked to Amy for an explanation. The best she could manage was, 'Maybe Hannibal fell out of the saddle back in the hills when we weren't looking.'

Stryker grinned at Dexter and said, 'Looks like we got us a handful of goofballs, Eddie . . .'

Without warning, the foreman suddenly spun around, lashing out with a reeling right hook. Murdock gingerly ducked the blow, and B.A. took it squarely on the jaw. Stryker's hand fared worse then B.A.'s face, and as the two men fell on one another for hand-to-hand combat, the other men followed their cue, turning the street into a wild, free-for-all brawl. Shelly was about to join in, but Daniel reached out and grabbed him by his shirt, keeping him in the land rover. With his arm in a bandage, he was wary of entering the fracas himself, and he was relieved to find that it didn't seem he'd be needed. The A-Team was far more in its element than the rustlers, who might have had the upper hand if they had stayed in their jeeps and tried to run Hannibal and the others over. As it was, no more than a few minutes went by before Stryker, representing the last foe still on his feet, took a left to the stomach and doubled over, the wind knocked out of him. B.A. grabbed him by the back of his collar and escorted him gruffly to his jeep, where Dexter was already slumped in the passenger seat. As Hannibal helped B.A. deposit Stryker behind the wheel, he laid out an ultimatum for any of the men who might be conscious enough to hear it. 'Inform Mister Carter that he's out of the horse-rustling business. No more of those mustangs are leaving that valley.'

Nobody in the two jeeps was in a position to argue, save for Lane Carter. She had viewed the drubbing of her uncle's men with horrified fascination, and now she stared at Hannibal and said, 'I don't know who you people think you are, but there's been a mistake here. My uncle is *not* a horse rustler, and once he hears about this fight here, you can bet he'll have the authorities after you on charges of assault and battery.'

'I'd suggest you look into the facts before you decide who's the villians around here, miss,' Hannibal said, rubbing at his sore knuckles.

'I'll do just that,' Lane huffed, moving over to drive the jeep she was in. Dexter came to before Stryker, so he took over the wheel of the other vehicle, casting a hateful glance at the A-Team through his blackening eyes.

Before Lane could drive off, Face dusted himself off and hurried over to her jeep, prying a bullet out of his gun. Tossing it to her, he called out, with a wink, 'It should be gold, but . . . well, you get the point.'

'Not really,' Lane said coldly, letting the bullet drop inside the jeep. Shifting gears, she pulled away to the accompaniment of groans from the men riding with her, whose bruised limbs ached anew everytime the jeep bounded over a rut in the road. Dexter followed close behind, raising a wake of dust. On the sidewalks, onlookers went back about their business, leaving the A-Team alone with the occupants of Daniel's land rover.

'I think things are going to get real interesting, real soon,' Daniel mumbled cautiously, watching the two jeeps turn a corner and head down the dirt road leading to Bus Carter's ranch, located a dozen miles away, up in the hills.

'It usually does,' Amy told him. 'Once the A-Team starts playing its hand, it usually does . . .'

SEVENTEEN

Bus Carter had three different residences on his land. Miles to the north, in the more mountainous territory, he had a nineteen-room log cabin overlooking a manmade lake stocked with the largest trout to be found in all of Arizona. Along the forest land bordering a National park to the east, a relatively small five-room hunting lodge was situated on a sprawling knoll that sported more species of wildflowers than any comparable area in the southwest, botanical gardens excluded. These two properties were viewed as retreats for Bus, and it was uncommon when he spent more than a few weeks at either one during any given year. The place he called home the rest of the time was the Bent Oak Ranch, a sprawling estate that was also the base of operations for the cattle business that was the lifeblood of his financial empire. Besides the split-level, seventy-eight room ranch house and the numerous farm buildings and feed bins, there was also his pride and joy, a personally-owned train yard, equipped with a vintage steam engine and enough railcars to ship his cattle to marketplace in one move and on the spur of the moment, allowing him to take advantage of market fluctuations.

After his ritual breakfast of hash-browns, two poached eggs, three links of sausage, and the latest edition of the Wall Street Journal, Bus Carter got up from the kitchen table overlooking the corral, downing the last few drops of his coffee. He was middle-aged, but daily workouts kept his physique trim and muscular and a sprinkling of dye kept his hair the colour it had been before the onset of menopause. Patting his stomach with contentment, he ambled out the sliding glass door and walked past the patio to the corral, where his favourite niece was riding a tawny, black-maned horse around the inner perimeter. Lane Carter seemed to be handling the steed with consummate grace, but the perfectionist in Bus wouldn't allow him to refrain from offering criticism.

'Keep your knees in! Dig 'em in!' he shouted through his cupped hands as he leaned against the fence. 'And let up on the reins. Give him more lead . . .'

Lane followed her uncle's advice, and her riding became increasingly effortless. The horse galloped smoothly around the corral, passing a gateway that connected with another enclosed area, where there were countless fresh hoofprints but no sign of the horses that had made them. The stable doors leading into the second corral were closed.

'How am I doing?' Lane called out as she rode past her uncle.

'Much better now,' he encouraged her. As he continued to watch her admiringly, Phil Stryker emerged from the stables and circled around to Carter's side.

'I figure we'll make our move with the mustangs in a couple of hours,' Stryker told his boss. 'I'll lead 'em from the stables to the trainyard and we can load 'em up while Lane's on that shopping trip into town she was talking about.'

'How many we got?' Carter asked lazily. His wrath at Stryker for the foreman's blunders of the past few days was under control, in part because of the calming presence of his niece, who encouraged his good side.

'Enough for two boxcars,' Stryker said.

'Not bad, for a change.'

'Only problem is, we only got one empty on the train. Unless you want to pass on making that delivery to McGivers.'

'No,' Carter drawled, picking at his teeth with a long blade of dried grass. 'I promised him that beef by the time the market opened. Just send out the one boxcar of horses. Use our engine. I can have McGivers send a couple of his for the cattle.'

'What about the rest of the horses?'

'Keep 'em under wraps and we'll move 'em out this weekend.'

The two men watched Lane put her horse through its paces for a few moments more, then Stryker asked, 'What about these guys we told you about, Mister Carter?'

'What about them?' Carter said contemptuously. 'You want to avenge those shiners of yours, do it on your own time. I'm not going to waste my time worrying about a bunch of masked yahoos who think they're the High Plains Drifters.'

'The Range Riders,' Stryker corrected. 'You know, cloud of dust and fiery horse and the quest for justice on – '

'Enough, Stryker!' Carter interrupted, 'Next thing I know you're going to start singing the theme song from the old t.v. show.'

'I don't know that, I'm afraid,' Stryker said, missing his employer's sarcasm. 'I just don't think we should take them so lightly, Mister Carter. I mean, they specifically told us not to go shippin' off no more horses to the dog food – '

Bus sent the heel of his boot digging into Stryker's ankle, silencing the foreman as Lane rode her horse within earshot of their conversation. When she spotted Stryker, Lane's smile withered. Ignoring him, she dismounted and tethered the horse to the railing, then hopped the fence, giving her uncle a perfunctory kiss on the cheek.

'Uncle Bus, I'm through for today,' she said, kneading her lower back.

Carter was visibly disappointed. Discarding the half-chewed blade of grass, he murmured, 'I kept Sentinel ready for you all year, just waiting for you to come visit. Now you want to quit after riding him less than an hour . . .'

'I'm sorry, Uncle Bus, but I'm a little saddle sore, I guess,' she apologized. 'Somehow riding the horse trails in San Francisco just doesn't substitute for the real thing.'

'I told you . . . gotta grip with your knees,' Carter

reminded her. 'Do that and you won't have to worry about the sores so much.'

'I know. I'll practise more on it later . . . maybe when I get back from shopping.'

'Good, I'm glad. Just keep thinking about it, though, okay?' her uncle advised. 'Grip with your knees.'

Trying to mend the rift between them, Stryker barged into the conversation. 'He's right, Lane. That's what keeps you from bouncin' around and hurtin' your . . . backside.'

The young woman gave Stryker a hard look, then turned and headed off for the patio, calling out to her uncle over her shoulder, 'I think I'll wash up and have some brunch before I go back into town.'

'Fine.' Carter waited until his niece had cleared the patio and disappeared inside the mansion, then turned on Stryker. His voice was calm, nonchalant, but his eyes betrayed the warning that was couched in his words. 'My niece is a good girl, Stryker. Young, idealistic. You see, she might not understand the realities behind what those damned horses are doing to the grazing land for my cattle. It bothers me that she'd have even the slightest inkling of what we're doing with the mustangs. Understood?'

'Sorry, Mister Carter,' Stryker said. 'That Injun kid just blew his mouth off before I could have a chance – '

'What's done is done, Stryker,' Carter interjected. 'The way she sees it, you've been rounding up the stray mustangs on reservation land behind my back. I told her I'd look into it.'

'But, Mister Carter, I'm only following your orders . . .'

Carter took a step forward, pressing his face to within an inch of Stryker's so that his foreman could smell the coffee and sausage on his breath as he whispered icily, 'I don't want any more dirt tracked around here. Period. You're paid a decent wage to exercise discretion when you work. I expect to get my money's worth out of you. Don't let me down, Stryker, because if you let me down, I'm going to have to let you down, too, and when I let someone down, they don't get back up.'

'I read you, Mister Carter,' Stryker said, his voice quavering lightly. 'Loud and clear. You've got nothing to worry about with me. Just tell me what you need done and I'll take it from there.'

Carter thought it over a while, then said, 'Well, the more I think about it, the more I'd like you to check up on those masked hoods after all. I want to know who they are, how good they are, and why they're here.'

Stryker saluted briskly, wincing as his thumb nudged the purplish swelling around his right eye. 'Yes, sir. I'll get right on it, send a couple of men down to Ohigai to check out the local places they could be staying at . . .'

'. . . if they're still around.'

'Somehow I got a feeling they are,' Stryker said. 'They're in cahoots with that Injun somehow, I know that much. They're hired help, I'll bet you anything.'

'The only help I'm worried about is the kind of a legal nature,' Carter reflected. 'If all he did was go rent a few gunslingers to try to scare us all off . . . well, we know how to handle them . . .'

EIGHTEEN

Howling Mad Murdock was down on his knees, one ear pressed to the hot, hard steel of a train rail. The gravel of the trackbed chomped at his knees, but he paid the pain no mind, for such was the way of the Range Rider. He would be impervious to pain, stoic in the face of hardship, calm in the face of disaster.

'No . . .' he mumbled, shifting his head to another section of track and pressing his other ear to the rail. No vibration was being transmitted along the line that he could sense, and he withdrew his head finally, turning to his horse, tethered to a nearby sapling. 'Nope. Are you sure, Thunder? I don't hear it, but if you're positive . . .'

The horse didn't respond, but B.A. did, lunging across the gravel and grabbing Murdock by the scruff of his collar, jerking him to his feet as he snarled, 'Okay, man, I've had it. I've warned you about talkin' to your invisible friends . . .'

Murdock wriggled free of captivity and pointed indignantly at his horse. 'Does he look invisible, I ask you? Huh? You can't see him?'

'I don't want you talkin' to nothin', got that? Invisible or not!'

'Well, I'm sorry!' Murdock preened righteously. 'But I am not the one with the bad attitude here.' Going over to his steed, Murdock stroked its mane as he continued to lecture B.A., 'If someone speaks to me I feel obliged to respond in kind, that's all.'

'That ain't a someone, Murdock!' B.A. fumed. 'It's a horse! And horses don't talk!'

B.A. regretted the words even as they were coming out

of his mouth, realizing too late that he'd cued Murdock for a command performance of the theme song to one of television's vintage comedies. Singing with sprightly abandon, Murdock knew the words by heart.

'A horse is a horse
Of course, of course.
And no one can talk
to a horse, of course.
That is, of course,
Unless the horse
Is the famous Mister Ed!'

The reviews of Murdock's singing talents came swiftly. Before he could launch into an encore, Murdock found his vocal ability severely restricted by the sudden application of ten ringed fingers around his neck. B.A. was in a rage, determined to shake Murdock as hard as he had to in order to get the man's shenanigans out of his system once and for all. Murdock, fearing for his life, brought his walkie-talkie up to his face and tried crying out for help, but all that could come forth was a hoarse, raspy howl with the coherency of a hacksaw cutting through a barrel of marbles.

'What's that, Murdock?' Face's voice came over the walkie-talkie speaker. 'Any sign of the train yet?'

'Yeammmfffffummmmahhhhh!'

Face and Hannibal were perched atop a rocky precipice a few hundred yards away, dressed for a good day's wrangling. Puffing on his cigar, Hannibal looked like he was trying out to be the new spokesman for a tobacco company reviving an image associated with the Old West. Peck seemed more conspicuous in his new outfit, the way John Travolta fans looked out-of-place when they'd swapped their disco duds for the look of urban cowboys.

Hearing the gargled reception coming over the walkie-talkie, Peck pressed the talk button and said, 'B.A., could you take your hands off Murdock's throat, please?'

There was a pause on the other end, during which Hannibal told Face, 'You know, maybe it was a mistake to have those two guys work together.'

'Nah,' Peck said, 'You know what they say about opposites attracting.'

'Yeah, but having B.A.'s hands attracted to Murdock's neck isn't what we're looking for.'

Murdock's voice finally came over the walkie-talkie, sounding less impeded than it had moments before. 'I don't hear anything on the tracks, but Ed says – '

'Ain't no train comin',' B.A.'s voice boomed over Murdock's on the speaker. 'And Ed don't say nothin'!'

Face lowered the walkie-talkie and looked back at Hannibal. 'Ed? Who's Ed?'

'Thunder's secret identity, I'd guess,' Hannibal said, taking out one of his pistols and nonchalantly inspecting it.

'You never let up, do you?' B.A. said, moving away from Murdock. 'Look, I'm goin' to the other side of the tracks, and I don't want you followin' me . . . that goes for your horse, too.'

'Hey, B.A., I'm crazy, that's all,' Murdock told him. 'I got a reputation to live up to.'

'Yeah, well bein' crazy ain't like bein' a golf pro. You don't gotta be practisin' it all the time!'

'Who says I practise?' Murdock retorted. 'I'm a natural!'

B.A. was halfway across the tracks when Murdock's horse suddenly reared its head back and let out a long, nervous snort through its flared nostrils. A second later, a distant toot announced the approach of a train. Incredulous, B.A. stopped on the tracks and looked at the horse, which was now nodding its head vigorously at Murdock.

'Man, this has gotta be a trick!'

'Think what you like, B.A.,' Murdock said with an indifferent shrug. Picking up the walkie-talkie, he put a quick call in to Face and Hannibal. 'She's coming, muchachos . . . and I'm not saying who told us . . .'

'We're on the air,' Face told Hannibal, edging toward the lip of the precipice. Straight down, a drop of more than thirty feet, were the tracks. Letting out a breath, he retreated from the edge.

'What's the matter, Face, you look a little green around the gills.'

'I'd feel a whole lot better if I had a parachute,' Peck confessed. 'Or at least inflatable boots.'

'No style in that,' Hannibal laughed, putting his revolver into the holster strapped to his hip. 'Give Amy a ring and make sure she's taking care of her end . . .'

Amy was halfway between the two teams, labouring over a stretch of tracks with a brush and bucket filled with a black, greasy substance with a repellent odour that would make a skunk's scent smell like an aphrodisiac in comparison. She'd already managed to layer a half-dozen sections of track with the goo, and she looked as if she were about to pass out from the toll the work had taken on her sinuses and stomach. In the process of brushing the tracks, she'd managed to get both hands and forearms covered with the substance, and when Face called in to her, she realized that she didn't have anything to wipe her hands off on.

'It's showtime, Amy. How goes it?'

Smearing the black grundge on her pants, Amy cleaned one hand enough to pick up the walkie-talkie. 'Great,' she informed Peck. 'I'm almost done. This stuff stinks to high heaven, Face. What kind of grease is it, anyway?'

There was no response at first, although Amy thought she heard a faint burst of suppressed laughter. Then Face told her, 'It's not grease, Amy.'

'What? Then what the hell is it?' Amy stared at the stains on her skin with a sudden revulsion. 'Face? . . . I asked you a question . . . Face!'

Face was too caught up in his own worries now to be

concerned with Amy's. Spotting a puff of smoke indicating the advance of the train, he warily clipped the walkie-talkie to his holster and joined Hannibal at the edge of the cliff.

'Still nervous, eh, Face?' Hannibal said.

'Hannibal, I really think this is about as flakey as it gets. We're not the Wild Bunch.'

'Don't worry, pal, it's not as tough as it looks.'

'That's a relief. Does that mean I'll just break half my limbs instead of all them?'

Hannibal took a last drag on his cigar, then carefully ground it under the heel of his boot before crouching and gesturing for Peck to do the same. 'I'm tellin' ya, Face, this is an absolute. It worked great in a movie I did once.'

'"The Giant Gila Monster Versus Billy The Kid", wasn't it?'

'You remember that one.'

'Who could forget it?'

The train's horn sounded again, this time much closer, and both men fell silent, waiting for their move.

Jake Babtany had been Bus Carter's engineer ever since the maiden run of his train system a few years before. He was a no-nonsense man with thick limbs and a full beard. No one on the ranch could remember ever seeing him wearing anything but his uniform – a sweat-stained t-shirt and soot-stained coveralls. For that matter, there weren't that many people who had ever seen the man outside of the locomotive itself. Wedded to his work, Jake would have been happy to stumble upon a job manning a train that never stopped rolling. When he was manning the controls of his engine, all was right with the world. Everything was simple and manageable. He had his destinations and his timetables and no other worries to muck up his day.

As he rounded the sharpest bend in the entire train line running from the Bent Oak Ranch down to the Mexican border, Jake reflexively slowed down the engine and pulled the antique stopwatch from the chest pocket of his coveralls.

'Right on schedule.' He said it like it was a prayer.

Once the curve had been negotiated and Jake was about to pick up his speed, he witnessed the first clue that there was going to be something different about today. Spotting Amy hunched over the tracks a hundred yards ahead of him, he tugged on the lanyard overhead, sounding a shrill whistle that sent the woman scrambling down the slight embankment supporting the tracks and off into the nearest brush.

Jake's instincts screamed for caution, and he refrained from accelerating the train as he would have under normal circumstances. Scanning the foliage for a glimpse of the woman who had been tinkering with the tracks, he spotted only an unattended land rover parked beneath a shady oak fifty feet from the rails.

'Something funny going on here,' Jake grumbled. 'Don't like it. Don't like it a bit.'

But it was too late for him to do much about it. Within a matter of seconds, the train was onto the greased tracks, which were so effectively lubricated that the massive wheels of the locomotive were unable to secure the traction necessary to maintain even the train's reduced speed. Although Jake tried to propel the engine faster, he only succeeded in getting the locomotive's wheels to spin in place. Most of the train's forward motion was a gift of its previous momentum.

'Something definitely isn't right,' Jake pronounced, his beard twitching with a vague show of emotion. 'I definitely don't like it one bit . . .'

As the train rolled slowly past the stone facing of the cliffs, Peck began to inch back from the precipice. 'Hannibal, I . . . aaaieeeeeee!'

Given a gentle shove by Hannibal, Peck flailed his arms in a travesty of flight as he plummeted down towards the first boxcar. Hannibal was right behind him, and both men landed on the roofs with solid thumps. Neither had executed the manoeuvre with any semblance of finesse, but they'd achieved the more important objectives of gaining access to the train without hurting themselves or tipping themselves off. The horses in the boxcar were making a fuss, but the commotion was something they'd been keeping up since leaving the corral miles back.

'See, Face, nothing to it!' Hannibal said as he carefully rose to his feet on the moving car. 'What'd I tell you?'

'You didn't tell me I'd be an inch shorter after that jump, for one thing,' Face countered. 'Okay, I'll take the front. You get the rear.'

'That's the plan,' Hannibal said, already on his way.

Jake leaned far out of the locomotive window for a good view of the doctored tracks that were foiling his progress. Once he saw that the engine had rolled pass the last of the greased rails, he began to pull his head back in so he could resume speed, but something poked against his skull that hadn't been there a few seconds before. It was a gun, and Templeton Peck was attached to it.

'You can put your hands on your head or in your pockets,' Face told Jake calmly as he climbed down into the engine compartment, 'but if you put them on any of the dials or levers around you, I'm not going to be very happy.'

'That'd make two of us,' Jake said, making a hat of his hands.

'Okay, tell you what, I'll be a nice guy.' Face pulled back the hammer on his gun and kept it pointed at Jake. 'You can drop your hands and put 'em to use braking this engine. Fair enough?'

'Gonna make me late on my schedule.'

'Yeah, I guess I am,' Face said. 'Sorry . . .'

At the back of the boxcar he'd landed on, Hannibal climbed down the rungs of an exterior ladder and waited for the train to slow down before dropping to the ground. As he walked along the car, which eventually rolled to a stop, B.A. and Murdock rode up to the train on their horses, followed by Amy in the land rover.

'Well done, team!' Hannibal told them. 'B.A., you wanna give me a hand with this door?'

B.A. dismounted and helped Hannibal unlock the massive side door of the box car, then shove it on its rollers until it slid clear of the opening that allowed the skittish mustangs to pour forth from within. Amy and Murdock had to move quickly to one side to avoid being trampled by the mass exodus of horseflesh. The four of them watched with admiration as the liberated steeds pounded their way back into the wilderness.

Murdock rode all the way up to the locomotive, then reared his stallion and fired his pistol into the air, in clear view of Face and Jake.

'And the mysterious Rider of the Range deals another triumphant blow for the rights of the oppressed!'

Jake stared at Murdock, who was now donning his mask, then looked to Face for an explanation.

'Don't ask,' Peck said.

'I won't.'

NINETEEN

'Who the hell ever heard of bandits on horseback in the nineteen-eighties?!'

Bus Carter was livid. Walking from his trainyard to the ranch-house, he gave his vocabulary of profanities a hearty workout, coming up with some well-seasoned outbursts that made even a hardened soul like Phil Stryker shudder. The foreman stayed at Carter's side, but kept himself at arm's length in case his boss wearied of verbal abuse and decided to vent his frustrations physically on the nearest target. He also kept his mouth shut, knowing from experience that until Carter calmed down, trying to talk with him would be like waving a cape in the face of a raging bull.

Eddie Dexter was sitting on the porch swing, but when he spotted the two other men approaching, he slipped out of the seat and stood at an approximation of attention.

'Jake's back awful early,' he said as Bus and Stryker were bounding up the front steps. 'How come?'

Dexter didn't know what hit him. The next thing he knew, he was sprawled out on the porch slats, rubbing his jaw where Carter had punched him before storming into the house. Dexter's head hurt, too, because he'd struck the swing on his way down. As he tried to reorient himself, Stryker came over to help him to his feet.

'All I said was – '

'Never mind, Eddie,' Stryker said. 'You were just at the wrong place at the wrong time.'

Dexter fumbled with his jaw, trying to get it rehinged to the point where he could talk without the pain bringing him to his knees. 'What the hell happened?'

'Jake got himself robbed on the way to the border,' Stryker explained. 'Those yahoos we rassled with in town sprung the mustangs and let 'em run back into the hills.'

'Ohhhhh.' Once the stars faded from Dexter's vision and the throbbing of his jaw had subsided, he and Stryker went inside. Carter was standing before the liquor cabinet, chasing down his second bourbon with a glass of branch water. He was surrounded by Remington sculptures of cow-punchers and rodeo riders, filling the panelled living room with the illusion of great activity, even if the only thing moving was Carter's drinking arm. The bourbon had already begun to soothe the land baron's nerves enough to let him move beyond his rage and onto the realm of plotting his next move. Hearing his henchmen enter the living room, he turned on them and spoke with cool deliberation.

'You get the men out there. You round up those stallions before they hit the grasslands and wipe out my herd. You get them and first thing tomorrow ship out them horses we still got corralled.'

'I'll get right on it, boss!' Stryker vowed.

Carter set down his glass and started up the winding staircase leading to the second floor. Three steps up, he paused and looked back at the men, adding, 'And find those bastards who think they can make a fool of Bus Carter!'

Dexter took a nervous step forward and volunteered, 'We checked all the hotels over in Ohigai, and I got a man watching the reservation. If they go there, we'll have 'em in no time. But if they're just out camping somewhere, we're talking hundreds of thousands of acres . . .'

'I don't care!' Carter rejoined. 'Take the chopper if you have to. Just find them or you'll be on the way to the slaughterhouse along with the next batch of horses!'

Carter turned his back on his men and bounded the rest of the way up the steps. As he started down the upstairs hallway to his study, the door to one of the guest rooms opened and Lane peered out, looking as if she'd just been awakened from a nap. A terrycloth bathrobe was all she wore over her nightgown and her hair was in disarray.

'I heard shouting, Uncle Bus. Is something wrong?'

'Oh, howdy, Lane,' Carter said lamely, forcing a smile. 'Just some business problems. Sorry I woke you.'

'That's okay. I should have been up hours ago.'

'Nonsense. You're here to rest. Go on back to bed. Maybe I'll take you into Phoenix tonight for supper,' Carter said. 'Would you like that?'

Lane nodded. 'You've got yourself a deal, Uncle Bus.'

Carter kept his smile until Lane disappeared back inside her room, then scowled his way into his study, closing the door behind him.

'I'll have those bastards' hides when I get ahold of them,' he swore under his breath as he opened the lid of the humidor on his desk and pulled out a cigar.

'Thanks,' someone suddenly said, swivelling around in Carter's desk chair and taking the cigar out of the dumbfounded man's hand. 'Don't mind if I do.'

'What are you doing in here?' Carter demanded, trying to identify the man in his chair, who was wearing a wide-brimmed Stetson that obscured his face. When Hannibal leaned back in the chair, only his eyes and the bridge of his nose showed above the bandana rigged across his lower features.

'Give you a hint?'

There was a side door that led out to a veranda overlooking the patio. Bus made a sudden motion toward it, but before he could make an escape, the door swung inward on him and he found himself face to face with Face, who wore a bandana as well and had a six-shooter aimed at Carter's gut.

'Going somewhere?' Peck asked.

'This is a stupid move, let me tell you,' Carter said as he backed into the study, raising his hands slightly to his sides. 'You guys are crazy to come here.'

'I agree,' Face said. 'I told you it was crazy, Hannibal.'

Hannibal shrugged. 'I wouldn't believe him.'

'He wouldn't believe me,' Face told Carter.

'What do you want?' Carter asked angrily.

Hannibal dragged a safety match across the desk. It flamed and he used it to light the cigar before declaring,

'We're here to file a grievance against the Carter Railway Line on behalf of the Wild Horses of America, West Coast Division.'

'Not to be confused with the Horses' Butts of America,' Peck added, 'of which we hear you're a member of long standing.'

'Funny boys,' Carter laughed coldly. 'You here to swap jokes, is that it?'

Hannibal shook his head. 'We would really appreciate it if you would stop harassing our loyal dues-paying membership. That includes, but is not limited to, mustangs, bays, fillies, colts, roans and yearlings.'

Carter edged closer to his desk until he was able to discreetly touch his toe against a button on the floor that activated a silent alarm system. Having tripped the alarm without discovery, Carter felt a surge of confidence flow through him, mixing nicely with the bourbon. He smiled thinly at Hannibal and Face.

'You guys are dead.'

Hannibal raised an eyebrow and checked his pulse while Face told Carter, 'You just don't seem to get the point. We're the ones making the threats. And believe what we say. We hear so much as a neigh from one of those mustangs out there and we'll be back to hogtie and brand you for good. Capish?'

'Now be a good boy and open your safe for us,' Hannibal said. 'We want any paperwork or bills you have from the slaughterhouse you do business with in Mexico.'

Carter opened his mouth to speak, but Face shook his head and cocked his gun. 'No more chit-chat, Bus ol' boy. Get the goods.'

The study was spacious and filled with oak furnishings and more Remington sculptures. Carter went over to a squat end table located next to an over-stuffed sofa. Triggering a half-hidden latch, he swung open a panel that exposed the thick steel door of a small safe.

'I told you it'd be in here,' Hannibal told Face.

'You win again,' Face conceded. 'That makes five bits I owe you.'

'We've also got a bet that you've got enough evidence stashed away to buy yourself a train trip to the state pen. Don't let me down, Carter.'

Crouched before the safe, Carter slowly opened the door once he'd twirled the combination. After checking to see how closely he was being watched, he reached into the safe, where several files and ledgers were haphazardly stacked. There was also a .22 calibre pistol secreted in a side compartment, and Carter blocked it from view with his body as he handed the documents to Peck, who was standing right behind him.

Peck lowered his gun, letting Hannibal stand guard while he skimmed through the material Carter had given him. 'Bingo,' he said, withdrawing a small account book. '"The Puppy Love Dog Food Company in Ensenda." Looks like I owe you another fifty cents, Hannibal.'

Hannibal was about to congratulate Carter on helping him win the bet when Carter suddenly whipped out his .22 and took aim at Peck. Before he could get a shot off, though, Hannibal sent a bullet flying at Carter, who promptly dropped his gun and grabbed at his hand, wincing with pain.

'Great shot, Hannibal,' Peck said as he retrieved Carter's weapon.

'I was aiming for his shoulder,' Hannibal admitted. 'How ya doin', Carter? I hope I didn't get your money-counting finger.'

Carter's hand was bleeding, but a signet ring had absorbed most of the bullet's blow, leaving him with a mere flesh wound on his right pinkie. He grabbed a handkerchief from his pocket to staunch the flow of blood as he glared at Hannibal.

'You're gonna regret that, cowboy.'

'There you go again, Bus, making idle threats again – '

'If there's one thing I'm not, cowboy,' Carter cut in, 'it's idle . . .'

TWENTY

There was a first-aid kit in the bathroom adjacent to the study, and while Carter treated his wound under Peck's steady surveillance, Hannibal moved around the desk and knelt down before the open safe.

'Well, let's have a look at what kind of goodies there are behind door number three,' he said, reaching into the enclosure.

'Who do you clowns work for?' Carter asked, wrapping gauze around his fingers. 'Can't be just that Injun. You must be in with the Lugansk brothers, right? They send you out from San Antonio to put a little scare into me, is that it?'

'The Lugansk brothers?' Hannibal said. 'Sounds like a Russian mafia to me. Or maybe a pair of accordionists I could hire out for a polka party.'

'Don't play dumb with me, cowboy.'

'Okay, okay,' Hannibal said, perusing one of the ledgers from the safe. 'I'll level with you. The Lugansk brothers are your connection in Kansas City when it comes time to turn your cattle into hamburger. They twist arms to make sure you get the best price per head you can when your train comes to town. How am I doing so far?'

Hannibal had surmised this theory from a few ledger entries and billing receipts, and from Carter's sudden silence, he guessed he'd struck a nerve, if not a bullseye. Peck was feeling adventurous, so he joined in the speculation.

'Maybe you've been thinking of switching allegiances lately, making the brothers nervous. And when the Lugansk brothers get nervous, somebody usually ends up being wrung through the sausage grinder. But you already know about that, don't you, Bus . . . which reminds me. Why do they call you Bus, anyway? What's it short for? Buster?'

The anger slowly seeped from Carter's face, and he slumped back leisurely on the sofa, offering a poker player's smile at his two captors. 'Okay, boys, now that you've had your fun, I'm afraid the game's over.'

'Oh, is that a fact?' Hannibal said, still browsing through the contents of Carter's safe. 'So soon?'

'Not soon enough,' Carter said. His gaze had shifted to the side door leading to the veranda, and he gave a short, imperceptible nod. Peck picked up on the gesture, and his observance saved his life, as it allowed him to duck sharply to one side as Phil Stryker came barrelling in through the door, gun blazing. Bullets whizzed through the air where Face had been sitting, knocking shards of marble from the base of the Remington behind him.

Peck had set Carter's .22 on the edge of the desk, and Bus grabbed for it as he scrambled for cover during the flurry of gunfire exchanged between Stryker, Peck, and Hannibal, who was now crouched into a crawlspace between the safe and the sofa. Stryker recoiled from Peck's shots, taking refuge outside the doorway and pumping an occasional dose of lead in the direction of his enemies. Over his shoulder, he called down to Dexter, 'Come on up! We got ourselves a pair of sitting ducks!'

Behind his desk, Carter crawled stealthily from one side to the other, then carefully peered around the corner. To his surprise, he found that he had a clear shot at Hannibal, whose attention was focused on Stryker. The ranch owner slowly raised his .22, drawing bead on his target.

As he was about to squeeze the trigger, the main door to the study opened inward and Lane Carter whisked into the room, shrieking, 'Uncle Bus!'

Hannibal, expecting the new arrival to be Dexter, jolted to one side to get out of target range, at the same time removing himself from Carter's view.

'Get out of here, Lane!' the woman's uncle roared.

Lane was startled, and during the moment's confusion while she stood in the middle of the room, Hannibal saw an opportunity for escape and sprang from his hiding place. Stryker fired a futile shot at him, devaluing another statue. Hostage in hand, Hannibal backed up behind Lane, using her for a shield.

'Go ahead, Carter, try your luck,' he taunted.

'Hold it!' Carter shouted over his shoulder at Stryker. 'Hold your fire!'

Peck was close enough to Hannibal and Lane to take advantage of the proximity. He rose to his feet and crowded in behind Hannibal.

'Tell your goon on the veranda to drop his gun and come inside,' Hannibal told Carter. 'With all this smoke in here, we think we'll step out for a bit of fresh air.'

'You heard him!' Carter shouted to Stryker.

'But, boss, we got 'em dead to rights! You can't – '

'Drop your gun and get in here, damn you!'

'Right.' Stryker reluctantly set his gun on the outside tiles, then stepped into the study. At the same time, Dexter appeared in the other doorway, gun in hand.

'Don't even think it,' Hannibal called out, spotting him.

'Do what he says, Dexter.' Carter set his own .22 on top of his desk and moved away from it, eyeing Hannibal with the purest form of antipathy. 'I'm warning you right now. Harm my niece and you'll be sorry you were ever born.'

'Oh, that's really touching, Carter,' Hannibal said. 'I know a few horses who could say the same to you.'

As Hannibal and Peck guided Lane to the side doorway leading to the veranda, Peck told Carter and his men, 'Sorry we have to shoot and run, but it is kind of Miss Carter to escort us out.'

TWENTY-ONE

Because Dexter had been called upstairs by Stryker during the initial phase of the short-lived siege in Carter's office, the grounds surrounding the ranch house had been left unguarded, and once Hannibal and Peck had led their hostage down the wrought iron staircase leading from the veranda, they were able to make their way to the nearby orange grove unmolested. There, tied to one of the trees, were the two horses Hannibal and Peck had ridden to the ranch.

'Upsy Daisy,' Peck said, releasing his grip on Lane and gesturing to the saddle. 'You and I are doubling on this one. I hope you don't mind.'

'Of course I mind!' Lane said, fear showing through the supposed tenacity of her words. 'I demand that you let me go and turn yourselves in to my uncle before this gets any more out of hand!'

'That's not likely to happen, Miss Carter,' Hannibal informed her. 'For the time being, why don't you humour us and mount up so we can be moving? You'll find we're perfect gentlemen when we aren't provoked.'

'You expect me to believe that?' Lane cried out. 'First I see you trading punches with my uncle's men in town, and now you're bullying your way around with guns and using me like I was a poker chip. If you're gentlemen, I'm the Queen of England.'

'Listen, your highness,' Face said firmly. 'We'll give you a count to ten. If you aren't in the saddle by then, we'll have to bind you and fling you over Trigger's back like an extra blanket. The choice is yours. Ten . . . nine . . . eight . . . seven . . . six . . . five . . . four . . .'

'All right, all right!' Exasperated, Lane raised one foot into the stirrup, then pulled herself up onto the saddle.

'And no funny business,' Peck advised as he climbed up, taking up position in front of her so that he could commandeer the reins.

'She isn't going to have time to do anything but hold on for dear life,' Hannibal said, pointing over Peck's shoulder, 'because we've got ourselves some rough riding ahead of us.'

Peck glanced back and saw one of the ranch jeeps screeching around the corner, then straightening its course toward the orchard. Whistling, he slapped the reins to get his horse going, shouting out to Hannibal, 'You lead and I'll follow. With Miss Carter as their only target we probably won't have to worry about catching bullets in the back.'

Leaning low and forward in the saddle, Hannibal avoided the low-hanging branches of the orange trees he was trying to manoeuvre his horse through, cutting a course along a rambling route determined solely on the objective of travelling wherever the trees grew so close together that the jeep couldn't follow. Even Peck had a hard time keeping up with the sudden shifts in direction and contending with branches that would slap back in his face after Hannibal had brushed them out of his way. The unpredictability of their flight course kept Lane from escaping, though, because whenever she would tell herself she was ready to let go of Peck and leap from the horse, they would take a sharp turn and she would be forced to cling to her captor to keep from being thrown clear in the other direction. She finally gave up any hopes of immediate freedom and decided to wait for a more opportune moment to make her move.

Although the jeep was not able to take up a direct pursuit, Dexter was able to race along the periphery of the orchard and venture down the wider rows of trees to stay in sight of the riders, who Stryker kept track of by standing up in the passenger seat and peering over the top of the windshield.

'Go right the first chance you get!' Stryker howled to Dexter. 'They're cutting in towards the hills!'

Dexter switched his foot from the accelerator to the brake, brodying the jeep sideways and kicking up divots of soil as he changed course and then barrelled through a gauntlet of ripe trees filling the air with the smell of citrus. Up ahead, the two horses were galloping at full pace. Lane turned and looked back at the men in the jeep, her face a cipher of mixed emotions.

'Faster, Dexter!' Stryker encouraged. 'Dagnabit, we'll catch those sombreros yet!'

'I've got this sucker floored!' Dexter yelled over the roar of the engine, bobbing in his seat as the jeep bounded over the uneven terrain, closing the gap between them and the others.

Hannibal heard the jeep gaining on them and hazarded a glance behind him, letting out a curse of frustration. When he turned his attention back to the way before him, though, a smile came to his face. They were almost at the edge of the orchard, and a fence of roughsawn wood formed the boundary between cultivated land and the wide open spaces of the foothills.

'It's jumpin' time, pardner,' Hannibal told his horse, digging his heels into the beast's hindquarters.

'What's he doing?!' Peck cried out, seeing Hannibal vault over the fence astride his horse. 'He expects us to do *that*?'

'We'll never make it,' Lane told him. 'Slow down or we'll be done for!'

Peck had less than three seconds to think it over. 'I think you're bluffing,' he finally told Lane, gripping the reins tightly and guiding his horse towards the fence. 'Here goes nothinnnnnnnnnng!'

Up the second horse leapt, clearing the top slat of the fence by inches, then landing on the run and continuing through the trampled grass marking the path left by Hannibal's mount.

'You could have killed us just then, I hope you realize,' Lane shouted in Peck's ear, still clinging to him tightly.

'Nah,' Peck said, oozing with a sudden rush of confidence. 'We got a horse that loves the jazz. We're all set . . .'

'What?'

'Never mind.'

The jeep neither had nor loved the jazz. With Dexter hunkering down behind the wheel, the vehicle crashed through the fence, crumpling its recently renovated front end, but not severely enough to deter its forward motion. Stryker, however, had been thrown clear during the collision, and he rolled through the knee-high grass like a piece of luggage being tested by a consumer advocate. He was quickly on his feet, barely scathed, and racing on foot after Dexter, shouting, 'Go, stay with the bastards! Don't let 'em get away!'

But Dexter hadn't heard his foreman's words. Slamming on the brakes, he almost taught the jeep how to do somersaults bringing it to a stop. Rising in his seat, he looked back at the frantically waving figure in the grass and called out, 'Hurry up, boss! We can still catch 'em!'

Stryker yelled something else, but Dexter still couldn't make it out. He cocked his head to one side and cupped a hand behind his ear. 'What's that, Stryker? I can't hear you!'

By the time Stryker caught up with his underling, he was in a black rage. Without explanation, he grabbed Dexter by the shirt and jerked him out of the jeep, which continued to rev in idle. 'Idiot!' he spat, throwing the jeep into gear and racing off after the two horses, which had almost cleared the first ridgeline by now. There was a road a dozen yards to his right, and he raced for it, hoping to make up the lost ground on a smooth surface. Coaxing the accelerator to the floor, he pushed the speedometer to three figures, but it was to no avail. By the time he reached the ridge, the horses were nowhere to be seen.

'Damn,' Stryker swore, slowing the jeep down. 'Damn and double damn . . .'

TWENTY-TWO

Even though he was sure they'd given their pursuers the slip by riding down a narrow defile reaching to the valley floor, Hannibal remained alert for the first sign of the jeep as he rode through the tall, bleached grass. His horse showed no signs of flagging under the toil it had been submitted to, but Peck's steed was wearing from the burden of two riders, and they were forced to slow down.

'No way is that jeep going to get back on our trail,' Peck told Hannibal. 'What say we give the nags a breather before my back gives out.'

'You should try gripping more with your knees,' Lane admonished. Since they'd reached the floor, she'd quit holding onto Peck, preferring to secure herself on the horse's back by grasping the saddle whenever necessary.

'Gripping with my knees?' Peck repeated suggestively. 'Sounds intriguing to me. Maybe you'd give me a demonstration?'

'How dare you!' Lane lashed out, trying to shove Face off the horse in her fury. 'You think you're attractive, but let me tell you, you make my skin crawl.'

Peck was taken by surprise with Lane's shove, but his cat-like reflexes allowed him to grab the saddlehorn and brace himself from falling. Swinging back up to an upright position, he grinned back at his prisoner. 'I don't supposed I'd rise in your estimation if I told you you're lovely when you're angry.'

'Jerks like you usually have a little more originality when they bandy their come-ons.'

'I think you better quit while you're ahead, Face,' Hannibal advised. He looked up at the sky, shielding his eyes from the mid-day sun. 'And as for the jeep, I'm not worried about that so much now. It's that helicopter we rode by on the way to the ranch that's got me worried.'

'If we hear it, all we have to do is ride under the nearest oak,' Face said. 'They'd never spot us . . .'

'Yeah, well we're a long way from the nearest oak,' Hannibal countered, tugging his reins to one side. 'I think we'll head over to the hills there on the right and then walk the horses up to where the trees are thickest.'

'My horse loves you for that idea,' Face said, following closely behind Hannibal.

Halfway to the first rise, Hannibal pointed to the ground, which bore the marks of unshod hooves. 'Looks like fairly fresh tracks. Maybe we'll be doing some horse-sitting before the day's out.'

'If my horse doesn't sit soon, it's going to go on strike, that's all I know,' Peck said, giving the steed a pacifying pat on the side of its head.

Once they'd reached a path that led up through a clump of weed-strewn boulders, Hannibal and Peck both dismounted and started leading their horses up the incline. At Peck's insistence, Lane remained in the saddle, the better to be kept in view of both men, who were constantly on the lookout for what they felt would be an inevitable attempt to escape. She was still playing for time, though, feeling that better opportunities lay ahead for getting away from her captors.

As he rounded the first bend leading up to the next elevation, Hannibal led his horse past a jutting outgrowth overgrown with thick brush. Before he could clear the foliage, the twin barrels of a shotgun slid out from the heart of a bush and lighted menacingly on Hannibal's shoulder. Freezing, Hannibal slowly let his eyes turn in the direction of the man wielding the shotgun.

'Hey, Colonel!' It was Murdock. He broke clear of his concealment and stood upright, withdrawing his shotgun and saluting. 'Camp has been pitched and our perimeters are secure.'

'Good show, Murdock.'

'Depend on the Range Rider to watch the range.'

'Right. So you haven't spotted anyone sniffing around? Nothing out of the ordinary?'

Murdock shook his head. 'The mustangs ran by an hour back and Daniel just showed up with Shelly and some grub. They're still here. Otherwise, it's been real quiet.'

'I can imagine,' Face sniggered, 'especially without Thunder to keep you company.'

'If that wasn't bad enough,' Murdock complained, 'B.A. insulted Ed something awful and now he's not talking to anybody.'

'I know it's tough, Murdock, but you gotta keep your chin up,' Hannibal said. 'Now why don't you take a higher post and keep your eyes open for choppers. I got a feeling they're going to be looking for us from above before too long.'

'Will do, Colonel.'

As Murdock wheeled about and bounded uphill through the brush, Lane shook her head with disgust. 'You all need professional help,' she muttered.

'Lady, we *are* professional help,' Hannibal told her.

The retort kept Lane silent the rest of the way to the A-Team camp, located in a small clearing near the base of a cliff some fifty yards away. B.A. was seated on a decaying log, watching intently as Shelly demonstrated the proper technique for making a bow. A few yards away, Daniel was showing Amy how to use one. She pulled back the bow-string as far as she could, taking aim at a bullseye target tacked on to the trunk of the same dead tree that provided B.A. with his place to sit. When she let go of both the string and the arrow, Amy groaned with disappointment, watching the shaft thud into the trunk a good three feet from the target.

'It's not exactly coming naturally,' she told Daniel.

'It's like anything else,' Daniel replied, taking up position behind her. 'It takes practice and the right touch. Just like driving a golf ball or shooting skeet.'

'Or typing a story under a tight deadline.'

'I guess so.' Daniel put his free hand over Amy's as she

nocked another arrow, coaching, 'First of all, you have to keep this arm straight and crook your elbow.'

As Amy was adjusting her stance, she and Daniel spotted Hannibal and Peck leading their horses to the campsite. Amy took particular note of Peck as he tried to help Lane down from his horse. The other woman kicked Peck's hand away and dismounted on her own.

'The well's never dry with you, is it, Face,' Amy called out drolly.

'Look who's talking,' Face said, staring at Amy and Daniel, who were still caught up in their instructional embrace. 'I saw you two as we rode up. Honestly, Amy, if I tried to give you pointers on how to shoot a bow and arrow, you'd be all over me for rampant chauvinism.'

'Since you don't know how in the first place, it probably would be,' Amy said.

'Touché!' Lane seconded. 'Nice to know I'm not the only one who can see through this smoothy.'

'And who are you, by the way?' Amy asked nonchalantly as she and Daniel put an end to their shooting lessons for the day.

'Let me introduce our new guest,' Hannibal said, tethering his horse. 'This is Miss Carter.'

'Bus Carter's niece?' Daniel exclaimed.

'That's right!' Lane confirmed. Staring defiantly at Hannibal, she went on, 'Just how long do you think you can get away with this?'

'With what?' Hannibal asked innocently.

'Holding me against my will.'

Hannibal looked at Lane, perplexed. 'Funny, I don't see anybody holding you, against your will or otherwise. You're free to go.' Moving over to the log, Hannibal opened a large brown bag and peered inside, sniffing. 'Mmmmmmmm, burgers and fries. True trail food.'

'We grabbed some take-out on the way here,' Shelly explained.

'Take-out hamburgers,' Face said, walking over for his ration of the food. 'You're really destroying my image of life on the reservation.'

Hannibal checked the bag, then told Lane, 'Looks like you've got your choice between a bacon cheeseburger or a – '

'You kidnapped me!' Lane cried out, baffled at the A-Team's seeming indifference to the gravity of their crime.

'Miss Lane, we did what we had to to keep us from getting shot and buried in a deep hole in the south forty of your uncle's spread,' Hannibal enlightened her between bites of burger. 'I realize you've got your family prejudices, but sooner or later you're going to have to realize it's your uncle who tweaks his moustache and ties young virgins to the railroad tracks. We're the good guys.'

'We'll let the law decide that,' Lane responded, crossing her arms.

'I don't think your uncle will call in the law,' Daniel Running Bear said. 'They might investigate too deeply and discover he's been rounding up the wild stallions and selling them illegally.'

'And that's just the tip of the iceberg, we've found out,' Peck told Daniel and Lane. 'He's gotten to where he is by more than mere hard work and good fortune.'

'I don't believe a word you're saying,' Lane asserted. 'On top of everything else, you have to resort to slander.'

'It's true,' Amy said. 'Like it or not, there's proof against Bus Carter that'll stand up in any court. Especially what he's doing with the wild horses.'

'But he just breaks in a few of them a year, that's all. I really don't see the harm in that. There's so many – '

'Your uncle's playing you for a chump, woman!' B.A. argued, leaping into the conversation with his characteristic bluntness. 'He sends his men out to gather the horses up and ship them out by train to Mexico so they can be turned into dog food!'

'I've heard that rumour once already,' Lane said. 'Even if it *was* happening, my uncle would never approve of it. His men must be doing it behind his back.'

Hannibal laughed lightly to himself as he finished his hamburger, then said, 'I bet you've still got a lot of naive ideas about Watergate, too, Miss Carter . . .'

'Why don't you take a look at this.' Peck reached into his pocket, withdrawing a few papers he'd managed to grab from Carter's ledgers before they'd made their hasty retreat. He handed them to Lane and watched her expression change as she recognized her uncle's handwriting on the account forms with the Puppy Love Dog Food Company, acknowledging receipt of nineteen horses less than a month ago.

'It can't be!' Lane gasped, unable to believe her eyes.

'Should make some interesting reading for your subscribers, Amy,' Face commented. As Lane continued to pour over the evidence against her uncle, Face glanced over at Shelly, noticing the weapon in the youth's hands. 'I see you got yourself a new bow. Watch how you use it, okay? I didn't bring that many jackets with me.'

'I was just showing B.A. how to make them so he can teach the kids in his day care centre,' Shelly said.

'Wonderful. I can see it now . . . kids shooting lunch apples off each other's heads, pretending to be William Tell.'

'No way I'd let that happen, sucker!' B.A. said. 'I'd have you come by and put the apple on your head for 'em to shoot at.'

'Oh, yeah? I'll have to remind my agent not to book me for that one . . .'

Lane had seen enough. Lowering the ledger entries, she whispered dejectedly, 'I tried to convince myself it was Stryker . . . I even went to Uncle Bus after I first heard about it. I guess maybe I thought he might be involved all along but just didn't want to admit it.'

'It's not a very flattering picture, I'll grant you that.' Hannibal crumpled his food wrapper into a ball, then tossed it in the take-out bag before going around to collect trash from the others. He then handed the bag to Lane and leapt back up onto his horse. 'Well, adios, kiddo. If you find a trashcan on your way home, drop that off, okay?'

'What? You're leaving?'

'So are you.' Hannibal said with a nod, pointing through the brush at a nearby pinnacle. 'If you head north and keep that peak in sight, you should run into your uncle's men sooner or later.'

'We'd give you a horse,' Face said, 'but then we'd have to rush ourselves moving on to new digs.'

'Aren't you worried I'll tell my uncle where your camp is . . . or what you look like?'

Hannibal shook his head. 'By the time you meet up with anybody, we'll be long gone. As for what we look like . . . we don't plan to be around long enough to get picked out of a line-up.'

Lane turned to walk, but after a few steps, she paused and looked back. 'I think I heard my uncle say there's still one more trainload of horses to be shipped out. He told Stryker that's the first thing he wants them to do. Of course, that was before he ran into you in his study.'

'Thanks for the tip,' Hannibal told her. 'Nice to know your heart's in the right place.'

'You still gotta walk home, though,' Peck said.

TWENTY-THREE

Once the A-Team had relocated their campsite a few miles from where they'd parted company with Lane, they spent a few hours mulling over various strategies and courses of action, taking into consideration a number of factors, ranging from the availability of supplies and munitions to the amount of time they felt they had to execute each given plan. It was late afternoon by the time they'd narrowed down their options and drawn up a list of items they'd need to implement them. Amy and Peck were chosen to make the run into town. They arrived in Ohigai just as the last tourist bus of the day was pulling out of the local Travel Lodge, bound for a scenic excursion through the desert on the way to Phoenix. Amy was driving her convertible while Peck scanned the storefronts for shops that would be most apt to have what they were looking for.

'Ah, there's a general supply store up there on the right,' Face said. 'That ought to do the trick.'

But Amy had other plans. Making a left turn, she pulled into a small shopping plaza and parked before a vacant phone booth. 'I want to call the paper and report in,' she said, going through her purse for change. Something was bothering her, and she wasn't making much of an effort to hide it.

'What about the store?' Face asked. 'You coming with me?'

'You're a big boy. I think you can cross the street on your own, don't you?'

'C'mon, Amy.' Peck tried turning on the charm. 'I could use your help. That was the plan . . .'

Amy got out of the car and headed for the phone booth, telling her counterpart, 'I'll bet you could use my help, but I'm through being suckered by you, Templeton Peck. Understood?'

'Aw, come on, this is just a straight little scam. It'll go down easy and get us everything we need without raising any suspicions.' When Amy entered the phone booth and closed the door, Peck hopped out of the car and came over, pressing his face against the glass so that his nose was absurdly flattened, trying to get a smile out of the woman who seemed so determined to ignore him. 'C'mon . . . Pretty please, pretty? I'm telling you, the brother-sister angle would really grease the skids on . . . oh, oh . . .'

Peck had unwittingly broached the topic that was at the root of the cold war between himself and Amy. Pausing before she dialled long-distance to LA, Amy looked at Peck. 'Are you going to tell me what was in that grease or not?'

Peck backed away slightly from the booth. 'I already did.'

'No, you didn't tell me,' Amy insisted. Sniffing her hands in the confined area of the booth, she made a sour face. 'I can still smell it. Level with me, Face!'

'Wellllll,' Face said, exhaling. 'It had a little of this – '

'– and a little of that. Yeah, that you told me. But that doesn't do it. I want to know the specific ingredients.' Amy waited patiently, but when it became clear that Peck wasn't going to disclose the information, she turned her back on him and started feeding coins into the phone and dialling the operator. 'Sorry, Face . . .'

'Look, if I told you what was in it, then you wouldn't help me for sure!'

'What!?' Amy glared at him. 'I want to know what was in that grease, and I want to know now!'

Face moved away from the booth, shaking his head. 'Oh, never mind. I think I can wrangle those supplies on my own after all. You go ahead with your call and I'll meet you back here in a bit.'

'And I'll be wanting an explanation when you get back, too!' An operator came on the line, and Amy turned her attention back to the phone.

There was no traffic, so Peck busied himself with skimming over the list of needed supplies as he started crossing the street. 'I guess I could pass myself off as an avant-garde sculptor,' he thought aloud. 'Yeah, that might work . . . unless I run into a realism freak, of course . . .'

Halfway across the street, Peck looked up from his list and promptly froze in place. Coming out of the local sheriff's office, less than a chip shot away, was none other than Colonel Decker and Lieutenant Crane.

'Oh boy,' Peck whispered to himself, taking a tentative step backwards, 'something tells me I should have worn my running shoes today.'

Peck swung around, turning his back to the military police officers, but not before they'd gotten a good glimpse of him.

'Colonel, that's Templeton Peck!' Crane shouted, breaking into a run.

'I knew we'd find 'em here!' Decker exclaimed, bringing up the rear and pumping his arms like pistons. 'Don't let him get away!'

Peck fled in the opposite direction of the shopping plaza where the convertible was parked, not wanting to draw Amy into the chase if it wasn't necessary. He sped past a service station, then ducked down a side alley, swerving to avoid running into a row of trash cans. Wanting to see if he'd eluded the officers, he shot a quick glance over his shoulder. At the same time, a teenage boy was coming out of a pet shop flanking the alley, toting a frisky Malamute pup on a leash. Peck was alerted by the dog's warning bark, but not in time to avoid a collision with the animal's owner.

'Hey!' the youth cried out as he toppled to the ground. Even though Peck had tangled himself in the dog's leash, he was able to fall clear of both the boy and his pet, landing on his knees and hands as if imitating a canine.

'Are you okay, kid?' he asked the youth, who seemed dazed.

'I think so.'

The Malamute, however, apparently took offence with Peck's impression of him, and it let out a fierce yelp before leaping at the older man, jaws snapping. Peck instinctively raised an arm to ward off the attack, and the animal's teeth closed in on the same sleeve that had been previously desecrated by Shelly's arrow.

'Oberon!' the boy shouted at his dog as he tried to regain hold of the leash. 'Down, boy!'

Decker and Crane were just turning into the alley. Peck saw them and quickly slipped out of his jacket, telling the Malamute, 'That's okay, Oby. It's all yours. I gotta run.'

As Oberon began clawing at the leather coat as well as chewing it, Face darted into the open door of a shop adjacent to the pet store. Before Decker and Crane would reach the same rear entrance, the dog became aware of their presence and decided they could provide more of a diversion than an unoccupied jacket. Trailing its leash behind it, the pup sprang forward, confronting the two men with fierce snarls that stopped them in their tracks. Having had his taste of coats for the day, Oberon went for the men's pants, forcing them to do some esoteric dance steps to make sure their legs didn't become part of the menu. The dog's owner, having an adolescent's typical response to authority figures, stood by and tried not to laugh too hard at the way Oberon had reduced Decker and Crane to a pair of slapstick comics.

Peck, in the meantime, realized that he'd strayed into a Western-wear clothes store, offering racks of designer items appropriate for every occasion from rodeo-riding to cowboy weddings. There was no one in the store but a clerk, who was munching on a sandwich at the sales counter as she read this week's issue of Celebrity magazine, trying to decide whether her ideal dream date was Tom Selleck or Morley Safer.

'Uh, miss . . . the dressing rooms?' Peck asked, arbitrarily snatching up a handful of belts from the nearest rack. Looking to the door, he could see through the glass that Decker and Crane were still being held at bay by the

Malamute, although the owner had now secured a grip on the leash and was trying to bring Oberon under control.

'You're only allowed three items at a time in the dressing rooms,' the clerk droned. 'You got five belts there.'

Peck put two belts back and said, 'I see where the rooms are, thanks.' Grabbing a ten dollar bill from his pocket, he tossed it hastily on the counter, adding, 'If anyone asks, you haven't seen me, right?'

The clerk inspected the bill, then slipped it into her pocket, nodding to Peck, who was already on his way to the back of the store, where there were two dressing stalls on either side of a three-way-mirror allowing customers to view themselves from all sides. The moment after Peck had ducked into one of the stalls, Decker and Crane came charging into the store, their pantlegs and nerves equally shredded.

'We're looking for a man who just came running in here a few seconds ago,' Decker told the clerk. 'Where is he?'

'Do I look like a private investigator?' the clerk replied snidely before turning her attention back to her magazine. 'You want to buy something, let me know and I'll be glad to help.'

'First that snot in the alley, now you,' Crane fumed. 'Doesn't anyone around here have respect for a uniform?'

'If someone cute's in one, maybe,' the clerk said, flipping pages. 'I bet Tom Selleck would look good in a uniform. I bet he'd look good in anything . . . or without anything . . .'

The officers left the clerk to her fantasies and began searching the store. Their quest soon led them to the dressing rooms, where they quickly began checking the stalls marked 'MEN'. Peck wasn't there, but while they were looking in them, there came a sudden scream across the way.

'Gotta be him!' Crane said, going for his gun.

Decker followed suit and both men converged on the women's dressing rooms. The stalls were arranged in such a way that they could see the legs and ankles of the woman who had screamed, along with her head and shoulders. Everything between was hidden behind a drawn curtain. From what the men could see of her, it looked like she had been interrupted between clothing changes.

'Are you all right?' Decker asked the woman, who seemed frantic as she clutched at the curtain to make sure it remained drawn.

'A . . . a man! He was coming after me, but then he dashed off through that window!' She was pointing at an opening next to her stall that led out to the back parking lot. 'My God, I thought he was going to kill me!'

'Was he armed?' Crane asked.

'He had three belts!'

'Damn!' Decker swore, venting his frustrations on a nearby mannequin, punching it in the stomach as he ran past and pushed his way out of the back door to the parking lot.

'He couldn't have much of a lead on us, sir,' Crane called out, taking off after Decker. Over his shoulder, he told the woman, 'Sorry you had to be put through this, ma'am.'

'I'll be okay.' Once the men were out of the store, the woman slowly let a smile bloom across her face. She pulled the curtain across the stall open, revealing herself to be wearing shorts and a halter top. Behind her, Templeton Peck was crouched into a ball on the bench built into the back wall.

'Are they out of here?' he whispered to the woman.

She peered out the window and saw Decker and Crane splitting up to check separate directions down a side street. 'Yeah, they're gone.'

Face lowered himself from his perch, sighing as he stretched his tensed muscles. 'Thanks, I really appreciate you trusting me like that.'

'Let's just say I liked your face.'

'Do I have a trusting face?'

'No . . . but I like it.'

'That's good enough for me . . .'

TWENTY-FOUR

As if the presence of Decker and Crane wasn't enough to cramp Peck's plans for securing supplies, he soon discovered that most of the town was swarming with Bus Carter's goons, who were placed at strategic locations to keep a lookout for any appearance by the A-Team. Even though he'd had a mask over his face during his encounters with Carter and his henchmen, Peck didn't want to risk showing himself, particularly since he noticed that all the men prowling the streets were armed and probably not about to rely on mere fisticuffs the next time they ran into him or his associates. Resorting to back alleys and side roads, Peck still had several close calls as he checked two different shops for the items Hannibal had requested. Of the eight essential supplies he'd set out to find, he was able to get his hands on three; an acetylene torch, a second-hand rivet gun, and a dozen sticks of dynamite. The torch and the rivet gun had been cash-and-carry purchases, but the explosives had been less easy to come by. Peck had had to sneak up on one of Carter's unattended jeeps, which contained the dynamite as well as other equipment that Carter planned to use to cut a clearing through a hillside for a new line of his personal railway.

Lugging his haul in a bulging grocery bag, Peck cautiously made his way back towards the shopping plaza where he'd left Amy. Unable to approach it from the front, he circled around back, then inched his way between the shrubs bordering the edge of the parking lot and the quaint chapel next door. When he came up next to the phone booth and poked his head above the shrub line,

Amy let out an involuntary shriek, almost dropping the receiver.

'No, no, I'm okay,' she told the man she was talking to back in LA, 'but I have to go. Something's come up. I'll be in touch soon . . . yes, I'm positive, I'm okay.' Once she hung up the phone, she rushed out of the booth, launching into Peck verbally. 'That was real cute, Face – '

'Shhhhhh.' Face lowered himself from view and spoke to her through the foliage. 'Listen, Amy, the MPs are sniffing around the town here along with some of Carter's men. Turn around real calm-like and sneak a glance at the post office across the street if you don't believe me.'

Amy pretended to brush some lint off her shoulder, at the same time sneaking a glance. 'It's one of the guys that tried blocking Daniel's land rover that time he was – '

'I know who he is!' Face hissed. 'Do you think he'd recognize you from then?'

Trying to catch on to Face's unspoken plan, she said, 'Probably not. I could pull my hair back and put on my sunglasses to be sure.'

'Good thinking. Now, what I need you to do is take this bag here . . .' Face said as he eased it out into the open, 'and put it in the car, as carefully as you can so you don't blow us all to kingdom come.'

'You got the dynamite, then?'

'Yes, ma'am. Then, if you could unlock the trunk and maybe walk to the other side of the parking lot and create a distraction for me.'

'You're going to crawl into the trunk?'

'It's our best chance. Start moving, and once you hear me slam the hood down, get back here and take off. We'll just have to hope that Decker clown didn't bother getting the make of your car and a description of you after we gave him the slip back in San Pedro.'

'How am I supposed to create a distraction?' Amy asked.

'Figure that the guy across the street is a hot-blooded chauvinist and take it from there,' Face whispered from the bush. 'I'm sure you'll think of something.'

'Right.' Amy went through her purse for a few barrettes and used them to put her hair up, then donned her sunglasses before reaching out for the loaded grocery bag. It barely moved when she tried lifting it at first. 'My God, Face, what's in here besides the dynamite?'

'The woes of mankind. I hope you're up to carrying them.'

Amy smirked as she repositioned herself, squatting down and putting her whole body into the effort of hoisting the bag and carting it over to the convertible. Once she'd managed to set it down in the passenger seat, she paused to catch her breath, panting, 'How about if I go over and pass out for him?'

'Too theatrical.'

'I was just kidding.'

'So was I. Get moving.'

Amy moved away from the convertible, keeping an eye on the man across the street, who was sitting on a bench in front of the post office, doing a bad job of pretending to read the Ohigai Daily. Amy was able to get his attention with a few swivels of her hips, and once she was across the parking lot, she raised one foot to a planter box to adjust her shoe, at the same time pulling up the leg of her pants to scratch an imaginary itch. Peering out through her sunglasses, she saw that her audience was being fully attentive to her performance.

'That's it, pal, just sit and drool like an idiot,' she muttered under her breath.

The man across the street stopped short of drooling, but otherwise seemed willing to oblige. Once she heard the trunk her convertible click shut, she moved away from the planter and approached a row of newspaper stands. In order not to draw suspicion, she purchased a copy of the local paper, then headed back for her car. She could feel the sentry's eyes on her, and when she cast a quick sidelong glance his way, she felt a twinge of alarm. The leering smile had left the man's face, replaced by a look of consternation that seemed like a precursor to recognition. To add to her concern, Decker and Crane suddenly appeared in front of her, entering the parking lot after having left the grounds of the chapel. Passing so close to the convertible that Crane almost brushed up against it, the two men gave no sign that they knew who owned it. Without so much as looking at Amy, they strode purposefully into the first shop in the plaza to continue their search for Peck.

'Close,' Amy murmured, 'Too close.'

Getting behind the wheel, she started up the convertible and backed out of her parking spot. Through her rear-view mirror she could see that the man across the street had risen from the bench and was still watching her. Rather than attempt a panicked retreat, Amy summoned her courage and decided to bluff her way out of the situation. Pulling her car up next to the kerb in front of the post office, she offered the man a polite smile.

'Excuse me, but I just came into town and I'm a little lost. I'm trying to get to the Bent Oak Ranch. It's owned by Bus Carter. I'm his niece's room-mate from college, and she invited me out to visit her on my way to see some other friends in Texas.'

'Oh!' the man said, the furrows vanishing from his brow. Relaxing considerably, he gave Amy directions, then asked her, 'You've never been to these parts before? I could swear you look familiar.'

Amy shook her head. 'Sorry.'

'Oh, well . . . you should be able to get to the ranch in an hour or so. Things might be a little hectic there, so you'd best be ready. Yer roomy ran into a spot of trouble today with some rowdies.'

'Oh, no! Nothing serious, I hope.'

'Could have been, but she's back now and she seems to be doin' okay!'

'Back from where?'

'You'll have to talk to her 'bout that, ma'am. Right now I got to get back to work.'

Amy thanked the man for his directions and drove off. Once she'd reached the end of the main street and had turned off onto the road leading into the hills, she smiled with satisfaction. 'Not bad, Allen,' she complimented herself. 'You can hold your own with the Team any time.'

A pounding behind her reminded Amy that Face was still in the trunk. Pulling off to the side of the road, she stopped the car and moved around to the rear, then calmly waited. A minute passed, then she heard Face pound on the trunk's hood again and cry out, 'Hey, Amy, what's the hold-up?'

'What was in the grease, Face?' Amy asked loudly.

'Amy . . . Amy, don't play games. The air's getting thin back here.'

'Well, it's plenty fresh out here.' Amy took a deep breath, then repeated, 'What was in the grease?'

'Aw come on! That's like asking Colonel Sanders what his twelve secret herbs and spices are!'

Amy fit the trunk key into the lock, but didn't turn it. 'I'm waiting, Face . . .'

'Okay, okay,' Face relented. 'I'll tell you, but first you have to let me out.'

'Nothing doing!'

'Look, Amy, either you let me out or I'll use this crowbar and pry my way out through the back seat.'

Amy thought it over. When Face started scraping the crowbar against the framework of the convertible, she quickly sprang the trunk open.

'Thank you very much,' Face said, crawling out.

'Now keep up your end of the bargain,' Amy said as they got into the front seat and she started the engine.

'Amy, there was nothing in that grease but the finest selection of choice petroleum lubricants . . . and a few necessary animal by-products.'

'A few what?!'

'You heard me. Now let's get going. We're already late.'

Amy guided the convertible back onto the road, shaking her head. 'I just saved your butt for the umpteenth time, and how do you show your appreciation? You make me cover myself with "animal byproducts"!'

'It's a dirty job, but somebody had to do it . . .'

'Don't talk to me, Templeton Peck.'

As Amy drove on, Peck picked up the daily paper she'd bought. A quarter-page advertisement jumped out at him and he smiled. 'Not to change the subject, but I think I just found the rest of our supplies . . .'

TWENTY-FIVE

The Southwest-Mexicali Railways Salvage Yard sprawled over three acres of desolate land located next to that company's train line. It was a rambling junkyard replete with the hulking frames of rusted boxcars, decrepit engines that had been picked clean of scavengeable parts, twisted rails, splintered ties, and a thousand other discarded items that had long-outlived their serviceability. Weeds proliferated amidst the metallic carnage, which was surrounded by a cyclone fence topped with barbed wire. Situated thirteen miles from Ohigai and forty miles from the next closest town, the salvage yard was not a place of booming activity. The ad in the Ohigai Daily that Peck had read pointed out that the business hours were Fridays and Saturdays from ten to five. The rest of the time, the yard was locked up and left to the elements. Accordingly, when the A-Team showed up an hour before sundown, all crammed into Amy's convertible, they had the place to themselves. Daniel Running Bear and his nephew Shelly arrived in the land rover just as the others were piling out of the car.

'You gotta be kiddin', Face!' B.A. said, staring through the gates. 'Nothin' here but a lotta big junk!'

As Peck walked up to the padlock securing the gates and began picking the tumblers with his locksmith's tools, he told B.A., 'Considering that the town's off-limits to us on account of Carter and those military snoops, plus the fact that it'd take at least a month to order the stuff we want from L. L. Bean, who don't stock it in the first place anyway, I'd say we've done rather well. Look on it as a challenge, B.A., a true test of your mettle.'

'My mettle don't need testing, sucker!'

'Well, I guess you'll have to test it anyway, B.A.,' Hannibal said, stoking up a cigar as he and Murdock opened the gates long enough for Amy and Daniel to drive into the yard. 'Carter's gonna be ready for us next time we strike, so we're gonna need a hole card for two to use on 'em. You should be thankful Face was able to at least get you the torch and rivet gun. I'd hate to see you out here trying to work magic with nothing but a bottle of super glue.'

B.A. grunted disconsolately as he followed Peck into the confines of the yard and the gates were closed behind them.

'We've got night lights and snacks galore, B.A.,' Face said. 'What say we all just get into the spirit of things and make a party of this?'

B.A. shot Face a glance that spoke a thousand words, none of them festive. The four men walked down the dirt road running through the yard, eyeing the refuse around them for anything that might come in handy. Amy and Daniel drove on ahead until their vehicles were beyond sight from anyone who might choose to pass by on the main road.

'Okay, our top priority is something we can transform into an all-terrain vehicle,' Hannibal said, tapping ash and trampling it underfoot. Straying from the path, he pushed his way through some knee-high weeds and signalled for the others to follow him. 'What about this antique?'

Murdock, Face, Hannibal and B.A. all gathered around a weather-worn handcar that looked as if it might have been a major innovation during the silent film era. There was more rust visible than metal, and the vehicle was straddling crosswise the set of tracks by which it had been rolled into the yard years before and left to rot.

'That ain't no ATV,' B.A. said.

'The important thing to remember is we want something that can cover the same ground as the train,' Face reminded B.A.

'Only thing this can cover is a corner of the junkyard, man.'

'Oh, I don't know about that, B.A.,' Hannibal argued. He slowly circled the handcar, bending over or rising on his tiptoes as needed to effectively complete his inspection. 'I think we could get this baby on the tracks and ready to roll with a little work. It's got a good, solid frame, too. That's a must. What do you guys say?'

As the others continued to stare at the handcart, Murdock said, 'Mister Ed could tell you how to fix it, B.A.' When Baracus reeled about and flashed a warning fist at him, Murdock stuck his nose in the air and added, 'But he won't, not after the way you've slighted him.'

'He ain't even here, fool!' B.A. retorted.

'Come on, B.A., what do you think?' Hannibal said.

Scowling, B.A. moved in for a closer look at the condition of the axles and wheels, swatting away cobwebs that got in his way. 'No way,' he proclaimed. 'We'd have to bust our butts just to move it back on the tracks, then there's no tellin' if it'd roll. I say we forget it, man.'

'How'd I know you were gonna say that?' Hannibal rolled up his sleeves and started flattening the weeds surrounding the section of track the cart rested on. 'We better start cracking, gents.'

'Hey, didn't you hear me, Hannibal?'

Hannibal nodded at B.A. 'Yeah, but I just love it when I'm playing against the house odds.'

'Man, you're one crazy dude, that's all I gotta say,' B.A. grumbled. 'Never do somethin' the easy way if you can help it, that's the way you operate, Hannibal.'

'That's right, B.A., and I wouldn't have it any other way. Neither would you. Admit it . . .'

B.A. cracked his knuckles and sighed, 'We got our work cut out for us.'

Daniel, Shelly, and Amy came over from where they had parked the cars and finished clearing the weeds around the handcart while Face went to get the tools out of Amy's trunk and Murdock teamed up with Hannibal to scour the grounds for other items they might need. When they found a large sheet of metal that had once been part of the lining for a refrigerated boxcar, they whistled B.A. over to help them carry it back to the handcart.

It took the combined weight of all those present, along with the use of makeshift levers and ramps, to get the hefty cart swung around and properly realigned on the tracks. When they tried pushing the vehicle down the rails, the rusted axles emitted twin, piercing screams that sent those closest to the wheels fleeing as they drew their hands to their ears.

'I think a lube job might be in order,' Hannibal said, wiping sweat from his brow.

Amy remarked sarcastically, 'Face has some animal byproducts that should do the trick.'

'Some what?' Hannibal said.

'Never mind.' Face started off, 'I'll go get the grease out of the trunk.'

'Might as well get the M-60 while you're at it,' Hannibal suggested. 'And if you find something lying around we could use to prop the gun on and still have some manoeuverability, bring that, too.'

'I'll help,' Murdock volunteered.

'Actually, I'll need you to help us rig this metal plate up in the front of the cart, Murdock,' Hannibal said. 'Amy, can you give Face a hand?'

Amy shrugged. 'Why not? We've been such a wonderful team all day, why spoil a good thing?'

'Atta girl!' Face said with mock enthusiasm. He and Amy left the others and started back to the convertible. The sun was in the midst of setting, and the descending twilight gave the salvage yard an eerie, almost haunting presence. As they were passing one of the abandoned boxcars, Face pointed to the hold, and Amy watched along with him as a steady stream of bats flitted out from the darkened interior to feast on the insects of the night air.

'This place gives me the creeps,' Amy shuddered. 'You and your brainstorms.'

'Creepy or not, you gotta admit it's the ideal location for what we're up to. I mean, not only do we have materials here, but from what I've seen of local maps, this is one of the few places where Carter's tracks merge with

Southwest-Mexicali's. All we gotta do is get that handcart rolling out of the yard and we're in business.'

'I guess you're right,' Amy conceded. 'Still, I'll be glad when this is all over. Oh, by the way, I forgot to tell you earlier . . . your girlfriend found her way home, apparently.'

'My girlfriend? . . . oh, you mean Lane?' Face had to laugh. 'I don't think that romance is going anywhere but down the toilet. Some people just don't respond to charm.'

'How would *you* know about that?' Amy snickered.

'Pithy today, aren't you, Amy?'

'Pithed off is more like it.' Reaching her convertible, Amy opened the trunk. 'I'll carry the M-60. The animal byproducts are all yours.'

'I'll never hear the end of that one, will I?' Face said as he removed the two buckets of black grease. They were sealed, but still the vile odour of the contents filled the air. Face set the buckets down on the ground and was about to close the trunk when he suddenly stopped and stared at something. 'Hey, that sure is a nice tripod stand you've got for your camera.'

'I don't like the way you said that, Face,' Amy said guardedly. 'What are you thinking? Whatever it is, the answer is no.'

Face acted as if he hadn't heard. He took the tripod out and unfolded it so that it would stand upright on its own. 'Looks like it's top of the line. Real heavy duty, huh?'

'It's not heavy enough to support an M-60, if that's what you're getting at.'

'Oh, you've tried it before, have you?'

'No, of course I haven't!'

'Well, you heard what Hannibal said . . .' Face looked from the tripod to the large automatic rifle cradled in Amy's arms.

'All right, all right!' Amy brought the gun over and Face helped her mount it on the tripod. It wasn't a custom fit, but it was clear that with a little tinkering the M-60 would rest securely enough on the tripod to be used. Amy took the rifle back and Face folded the tripod back up and tucked it under one arm while he used both hands to pick up the buckets of grease.

'It's all for a good cause, remember that, Amy.'

'Yeah, yeah,' Amy muttered as they headed back to rejoin the others. 'Sometimes I wonder why I didn't stick to transcribing wire copy.'

'No excitement, no thrills. You're a gal who likes gusto.'

'Thanks, Face, I needed that.'

Back at the tracks, Hannibal and Murdock were holding the large steel plate in place at the front end of the handcart while B.A. used the acetylene torch to weld it to the frame.

'Is it gonna hold, B.A.?' Hannibal asked.

'Could be,' B.A. said. 'We oughta pop some rivets into it to make sure, though. Gotta have some power to do that.'

Daniel and Shelly were holding gas lanterns on either side of B.A., helping to shed light on his work now that the skies were darkening. Shelly said, 'When we parked the car, I saw an outside outlet by the office.'

'And I've got extension cords in the land rover,' Daniel added. 'They're grounded, too . . .'

'That would work if it reaches that far,' B.A. said.

Amy and Face showed up to take Daniel and Shelly's places holding the lamps. When Hannibal spotted the tripod stand they'd brought, he smiled, 'Now why didn't I think of that? Good idea, Amy.'

'Thanks,' Amy said, trying not to look at Face.

B.A. was finished with his welding by the time Daniel and Shelly had run the extension cord from the salvage yard office to their work area. Before he loaded the rivet gun and put it to use, Amy and Face found a way to rig up the lamps so that they wouldn't have to hold them constantly. Hannibal and Murdock carefully let go of the steel plate and were encouraged when it held in place.

'Great!' Hannibal said, pleased. He looked up at the sky, where stars were winking into life around the vibrant glow of the moon. 'Looks like it'll stay light enough through the night for us to find our way around. I saw a nice spot just past the yard here that will be ideal for Operation Booby Trap. While B.A. does the riveting and Face greases things up, I want the rest of us to chip on the rest of the plan. With a little luck, we'll be done by dawn . . .'

TWENTY-SIX

Paranoia was the operative word when Bus Carter's train rolled out of Bent Oak Ranch and began its second trek toward the Mexican border in as many days. Jake Babtany had company this time around. Phil Stryker was riding with him inside the locomotive, and Eddie Dexter was one of five men stationed atop the coal car and boxcar behind it, armed and watching the territory around them for the first sign of any attempt by the A-Team to disrupt the train's progress.

'I dare 'em to try somethin' this time around,' Stryker said.

Slowly the engine built up its momentum, chugging along the tracks, chasing its shadow cast by the just-risen sun. There was a cloudless sky, and the air was still. A pair of hawks circled lazily above the hills, but otherwise there was no activity save for that of the train. It was almost too calm, and as the ranch fell from view, the sentries became increasingly wary. At one point a rustling in the brush alongside the tracks prompted a torrent of gunfire from Stryker and his men. The bullets wreaked havoc on a cluster of mesquite, flushing out a bewildered coyote, which yipped with terror as it scampered off into the foothills.

'Damn!' Stryker cursed, pulling his gun back in from the engine window. 'Missed 'im!'

'Six guys blast away and you can't hit a lousy coyote?' Jake clucked his tongue as he checked gauges and shovelled another load of fuel into the locomotive's vintage burner. 'Sure makes a guy feel like he's well-protected.'

'Hey, if that varmit woulda been one of them gang

members, we woulda had him lookin' like Swiss cheese,' Stryker insisted as he holstered his gun. 'You got my word on that.'

'Uh huh, sure thing, Phil.' Jake scratched his beard and looked out of the window. 'Well, you might get a chance to prove it, 'cause we're comin' up on the spot where they sprang the ambush yesterday.'

Stryker spotted the wall of stone rising adjacent to the tracks a hundred yards ahead and let his gaze drift up to the top of the formation. 'Doesn't look like anyone's up there now.'

'Didn't look like it yesterday, neither.'

Stryker and Jake were taking turns feeding the burners, and as Phil took the shovel back to the coal car, he called up to Dexter, 'Keep an eye on this clifftop we're comin' to. Anybody pokes their head into view, drill 'em!'

'My pleasure.' Dexter shifted his position, swinging his rifle up at an angle and lining his sights on the cliff. The man riding the coal car with him did the same, while the others atop the boxcar continued to inspect the ground level of the terrain around them, each of them anxious to redeem themselves for the fiasco with the coyote.

Tensions mounted as they drew nearer to the cliffs, but there was still no movement indicating that the A-Team was in the area. When the train rolled past the stone facing, the sound of its steam-driven pistons bounded loudly off the cliffs, but there were no other sounds or interruptions. They cleared the point without incident and began rounding a gradual bend that would take them past the salvage yard. It was then that Jake spotted the first sign of trouble.

'I'll be danged,' he muttered. 'Take a look at that, would you?'

'Where?' Stryker said, setting aside the shovel in favour of his gun.

'Straight ahead.' Jake pulled away from the window to let Stryker have a look, then reached for the lanyard and gave it the three short tugs that sounded a prearranged signal that the enemy had been sighted. Over the shrill blasts of the train's whistle, Jake intoned, 'Looks like we got ourselves some crazies going the wrong way on a one-way street . . .'

The A-Team's refurbished handcar was bound on a collision course with the oncoming train, looking every bit like the railway equivalent of David on his way to do battle with Goliath. Even the application of Peck's patented grease hadn't been able to fully subdue the friction of the axles, and each revolution of the car's wheels was accompanied by a steady, high-pitched squeal. A similar noise was given off as B.A. worked the hand pump that propelled the vehicle. He worked within an enclosed area formed by four walls of metal plating he and the others had fixed in place around the outer framework of the handcar. There was no roof, though, allowing a free flow of air to keep B.A. from losing his strength to excessive sweating. Hannibal rode with B.A., manning the M-60, which had been mounted on the tripod and secured in place at the front of the car so that the barrel projected from the top of the plate.

'Did I just hear train whistles or am I startin' to go goofy from all this work?' B.A. said between breaths, his muscles glistening as he pumped the lever with a steady rhythm.

'You heard right, B.A.,' Hannibal told him above the chirping of the car. 'Here they come . . . right on schedule.'

On the upswing, B.A. managed to peer over Hannibal's shoulder at the advancing train. 'Hey, man, they don't look like they're slowing down.'

Hannibal puffed his cigar confidently, swivelling the M-60 from side to side to make sure it wasn't catching on anything. 'They'll slow down. Just keep pumping, B.A.'

B.A. blinked the sweat from his eyes and bore down on the lever again, feeling the strain on his muscles, which had already been subjected to hours of work during the course of the night. He'd had two hours of sleep at one point, but he didn't feel as if it had done him any good. 'Now I know why they quit makin' these suckers and started usin' machines instead. Man, this is worse than boot camp!'

'You're doing fine, B.A.'

'B.A. pumped again and rechecked the position of the locomotive. 'I thought you said they'd slow down, Hannibal!'

'They have to,' Hannibal said with less assurance. 'That's all there is to it.'

'Tell *them* that!'

Hannibal didn't have to tell Jake Babtany anything. The engineer had spent too many loving hours maintaining the pristine exterior of his prized locomotive to even consider marring its surface by ramming into the metallic abberation rolling towards it. Within seconds after spotting the handcar, Jake was reaching for the necessary controls to cut the engine's power and apply the brakes.

Stryker, however, had other ideas.

'Keep a full head of steam, Jake.'

Jake's normally expressionless face was ruptured by a look of astonishment. 'Are you nuts?'

'I said keep going!' Stryker pushed past Jake and rammed the throttle forward. Spewing jets of steam, the engine spurted forward with increased speed, bearing down on the diminutive obstacle in its path.

B.A. noticed the change. 'They're going faster, Hannibal!' he shouted vehemently. 'They wanna make us look like pancakes!'

Hannibal's jaw hung open and his cigar fell from his lips as he stared at the face of the locomotive, which loomed closer each second. 'Son of a gun,' he whispered feebly, 'they're not stopping . . .'

'Man, we don't even have seat belts in this sucker!'

'Don't worry, B.A., Face'll come through for us!'

'I'm worrying!'

Hannibal looked off to the side of the tracks, where Peck was standing at a point halfway between the handcar and the onrushing locomotive. Barely hidden behind a stacked pile of tumbleweeds, he was feverishly attempting to turn the lever of a rebuilt switching mechanism he and Murdock had installed under B.A.'s supervision only a few hours before. There were missing teeth on the gears, though, and the switch jammed on Peck before it could do its job.

'No!' he spat, jerking the lever back and trying again. 'Catch this time, damn you!'

Apparently the mechanism liked it when Peck talked dirty. The gears meshed on the second try, and Peck was able to shift the course the train would take when it rushed past him. Instead of thundering straight ahead and ushering the handcar into oblivion, the locomotive was rerouted onto a rusty set of freshly-laid parallel tracks that dead-ended a hundred yards away into an unyielding rock formation.

'Whoah, Abigail!' Jake shouted inside the locomotive once he realized what had happened. With desperation, he reached out and jerked Stryker away from the train's controls, then tugged fiercely on the emergency brakes. Unlike the regular brakes, which worked more gradually, the emergency system was designed exclusively for immediate stops, and stop immediately the train did, spitting sparks from its locked wheels as they ground into the rails.

Jake was ready for the suddenness of the stop and braced himself, but Stryker lost his footing and teetered out the back of the engine, landing roughly in the coal bin. Elsewhere on the train, Dexter was clinging to the sides of the coal car and his sidekick had been shaken loose, falling roughly to the ground and knocking himself out. Half of the other marksmen had also been jarred from the boxcar by the abrupt stop, and while they too lost consciousness on impact, they were fortunate they hadn't lost their lives by falling into the path of the handcart, which B.A. continued to pump until it was alongside the train.

As B.A. moved away from the lever and crouched behind the protective plating, Hannibal swung the M-60 around and drew aim on the locomotive as he crouched low to make himself as inconspicuous a target as possible.

'Okay,' he called out to those aboard the train. 'Release the horses or we knock you down to Lionel size and put you under some prison warden's Christmas tree!'

Brushing soot off his clothes, Stryker peered out at the plated handcar, wondering what to do. Neither he nor his men had a clear shot at the men inside the reinforced walls.

'Back up, Jake,' he ordered. 'Hurry! We can get back on the main track and mow 'em down once we work the switch.'

Jake had his doubts about Stryker's plan, but he was in favour of any strategy that might get the locomotive beyond the range of Hannibal's M-60. Releasing the brakes, he grabbed for the throttle. The train began to roll in reverse, but before it had cleared more than a dozen feet, a sudden explosion ripped away an entire section of tracks between it and the main line, trapping it on the spur.

Up in the hills, Howling Mad Murdock moved away from the makeshift plunger he'd used to detonate the charges under the tracks and let out a cry worthy of his nickname. If he would have stripped down to a loincloth and beat his chest, he could have passed as Tarzan rather than the Range Rider.

Furious, Stryker waved his gun out the window of the engine and shouted, 'Okay, if you bastards want to play tough, we'll play tough!'

Stryker emptied his gun in the direction of the handcar, but the bullets pinged off the metal plating, leaving no more than slight dents. The riflemen on the roofs of the boxcar fared no better, although, from their higher perspective, two of them were able to send shots into the confines of the car, where they ricocheted off the inner walls, missing B.A. and Hannibal by scant inches.

'Jockey us back and forth, B.A.,' Hannibal said. 'Make it harder for 'em! I'll keep 'em busy for ya!'

As B.A. moved back to the lever and put it back to work, Hannibal squeezed the trigger of his M-60, stitching the sides of the train with hot lead. He didn't strike any of the men, but Jake was sickened by the desecration of his beloved locomotive. 'What did I ever do to them?' he sulked, moving away from the window.

Dexter scurried back into the hold of the coal car and began heaving large chunks of the black fuel like grenades over the walls of the handcar, in the hopes that a lucky toss might take out the M-60 or its operator. Just as he was about to launch a particularly large piece, Dexter spotted an arrow that had suddenly thunked into the hold. An arrow alone wouldn't have disturbed him excessively, but this shaft had a lit stick of dynamite attached to it, and the fuse was almost burned down all the way to the stick.

'What the . . .' Dexter was closer to the top of the car than he was to the dynamite, so instead of trying to throw out the stick, he ejected himself from the bin, landing on the ground away from the handcar just as the walls of the car bulged outward from the force of an explosion that sent pulverized coal dust flying into the air like black clouds.

Shelly had been responsible for the shot heard 'round the range, firing at the train from a ledge fifty yards away. Amy and Daniel were with him, readying another of the high-powered arrows.

'Good shot, Shelly,' Daniel told his nephew. 'Here, let's have an encore.'

Shelly sent another volley down at the train. This one missed its mark, but still created enough of a disturbance to send the men on the ground fleeing for the nearest cover away from the tracks without their weapons. Fearing that the next arrow might blow up the boxcar, one of the men on the roof quit firing at the handcar and climbed down from his perch. His partner stayed where he was, but he didn't seem all that determined to continue fighting the odds.

After another blast rocked the area of confrontation, Hannibal fired off his last round of ammunition, then shouted to those on and around the train, 'This is your last chance to drop your weapons and surrender while you're still in one piece!'

Any last vestige of resistance was shattered by the explosion of another rigged arrow, which almost ripped the roof off the boxcar. One by one, Carter's henchmen threw down their weapons and raised their arms as they emerged from cover.

Aboard the locomotive, Stryker witnessed the mass surrender, but couldn't bring himself to give up that easily.

Crouching low, he moved to the rear of the compartment, hoping to sneak out the back way and escape. However, once he'd backed down the outside ladder and reached the ground, he turned around and found his way blocked by Peck, who was armed with a .357 Magnum.

'Hi there!' Peck said cheerily. 'Don't be shy. Let's go join the rest of the party, okay?'

'You guys shoulda quit while you were ahead,' Stryker shot back sullenly as Peck relieved him of his gun and escorted him around the train to where the rest of Carter's men were being rounded up. Hannibal remained in the handcar, holding onto the M-60 as if it were still loaded, Both he and Peck knew better, though, and once he had Stryker back in the fold, Face went over to Hannibal and slipped him the Magnum.

'Good job, Face. You had me worried for a second.'

'Aw, come on, Hannibal, you knew I wouldn't let you down.'

'Maybe not you, but that switch lever was a few decades past its warranty.'

'I just had to know how to talk to it.'

'Right,' Hannibal drawled. 'Now how's about tending to the boxcar? I figure those horses must be itching to bust outta there after all this excitement.'

As Face headed back to the train, Hannibal looked to the hills and waved to Murdock and the trio who had handled the aerial bombardment. They all waved back, relieved to know that their work of the past night had produced the intended results.

The train wasn't going anywhere, but it still gave off enough noise that it was difficult for Peck to hear the horses inside the boxcar as he unfastened the latch to the sliding door. Once he shoved the door along its grooved runners, he found another reason why there had been no equestrian sounds inside the boxcar.

The horses weren't there.

In their place were the three jeeps of Carter's mobile fleet Their engines were running and men were behind the wheels. Stunned, Face had to lunge to one side to avoid being run down as the first of the jeeps surged forward, landing with a hard bounce on the ground. When the other two jeeps followed suit, each vehicle containing an armed rider as well as its driver, the A-Team realized that the balance of power had just taken a rude turn for the worse.

'C'mon, Face!' Hannibal shouted. 'We're outta here!'

Face bolted for the handcar, taking advantage of the shots Hannibal was firing at the jeepsters to keep them from gunning him down. Several of the would-be prisoners dropped their arms and tried to bring Peck down, but he threaded his way through them like a fullback showing off for hometown fans.

'Hit it, B.A.!' Hannibal cried out.

'I'm tryin'!' B.A. said, once more applying his weight to the cart's massive lever. Slowly the car began creaking back in the direction of the salvage yard. Face bounded up onto the tracks and Hannibal leaned over the plating to give him a hand. Peck grabbed for it and Hannibal pulled him aboard as bullets zinged around him.

'Looks like they were smarter than we gave them credit for,' Face said as he climbed into the shielded area of the handcart.

'That didn't take much,' Hannibal replied, firing another shot at their pursuers. The three jeeps were picking up speed and already flanking the handcart on both sides as the armed riders pummelled the plating with steady gunfire. Hannibal was forced to duck for cover, giving up their puny offence.

'Shelly's out of his magic arrows by my count, too,' Face said glumly, assessing the situation.

'We need more gas, B.A.!' Hannibal hollered.

'I'm goin' as fast as I can, damn it!' B.A. protested, huffing away at the lever. Face moved over and helped work the pump, increasing their acceleration negligibly.

'We ain't gonna make it!' B.A. groaned between swings.

'Who knows?' Face said, clinging to optimism. 'We still have the Range Rider as an ace up our sleeves.'

'We definitely ain't gonna make it!' B.A. reaffirmed.

Two of Carter's jeeps remained alongside the handcar

while the third forged ahead. The relentless fusillade of gunfire kept Hannibal from rising to a point where he could see what was going on. Crawling on all fours, he moved away from the M-60 and made his way to the other end of the car, where he was able to peek out through a vertical gap between two imperfectly matched sheets of metal plating.

'Oh, no . . . too bad we don't have brakes,' he said dismally, seeing that the lead jeep had just bounced up onto the tracks and stopped. Its driver and rider were jumping free as the handcart drifted towards it. Hannibal sounded a warning to B.A. and Peck, but even when they stopped working the lever, it was too late to prevent them from crashing into the stranded jeep. With a sick crunch, the two vehicles bit into one another and tumbled off the tracks like wrestling machines. By the time they came to a rest in a clogged heap, Hannibal, Peck, and B.A. had been tossed about and spat free of the wreckage. They were quickly surrounded by Stryker and the rest of Carter's men, who showed no signs of mercy in their eyes.

'I just hate it when a plan falls apart,' Hannibal moaned.

'There's gonna be more than a plan falling apart by the time we're through with you guys,' Stryker promised.

TWENTY-SEVEN

Jake Babtany surveyed the damage to the locomotive with a remorse that stretched his features like taffy left out in the sun. As he ran his fingers along the scarred surface, he winced upon contact with each bullethole as if the wound had been inflicted upon his own flesh.

'Poor Abigail,' he murmured hoarsely. 'Poor girl . . .'

Stryker was standing a few yards away, indulging Jake in his grief. But when the engineer continued to woefully caress the damaged frame, Carter's foreman felt his patience leaving him. 'My neck's on the line and he thinks he's the railroad's answer to Florence Nightingale,' he grumbled to himself. Raising his voice, he called out, 'Look, Jake, can the sucker still run or not?'

Jake nodded silently, taking a deep breath and trying to keep the mist in his eyes from growing into tears. He couldn't even bear to look at the roof of the boxcar or the hold of the coal bin, where the dynamite had created the worst damage.

'And what about the tracks?' Stryker asked. 'We gonna be able to get back on the main line?'

Jake sighed and trudged past the prisoners Stryker had taken into custody. If looks could kill, Jake would have been up for triple murder.

'Sorry, pal,' Hannibal said. 'I guess that's the price you gotta pay for running with the wrong circles.' He was tied up, sandwiched between Peck and B.A., who were similarly bound. Their spill from the sabotaged handcar had left them bruised, but not injured to the extent that they couldn't stand on their own and gaze into the bores of five different kinds of weapons holding them at bay.

Stryker left Dexter and the other men to guard the A-Team while he followed Jake to the rear of the boxcar for a look at the tracks that had been blown up earlier. Twisted lengths of steel rose at jagged angles from the rubble of demolished ties and stray dirt.

'Gonna have to replace that piece of rail,' Jake said. 'Otherwise we aren't going anywhere . . . Phil, did you see what they did to my train?'

'It's Carter's train, damn it!' Phil shouted. 'Quit your blamed moping and help us get outta this mess or the only trains you'll be running will be the kind kids play with in the basement. Savvy?'

Jake drilled Stryker with a dark stare, then turned his back on the foreman and went over to the ruptured tracks to calculate what would be needed to replace them. Stryker waved a few of his men over to help the engineer, then rejoined the captives.

'You guys sure know how to make a nuisance of yourselves,' he told them unpleasantly.

'We do our best,' Hannibal bragged.

Two men in one of the jeeps had been searching the area surrounding the tracks for anyone else who had participated in the second assault on the train, and when they returned, they had nothing to present to their boss but terse shakes of the head.

'The others musta got away,' one of them said. 'You want we should cut a wider circle lookin' for 'em?'

'No, they're probably long gone by now,' Stryker said. 'Go help Jake and the others piece together a new length of track so we can back this train off the spur and get about our business.'

'That's gonna take some time . . .'

'Then get moving!' Stryker shouted. 'We still gotta get back to the ranch and load up them mustangs, providing the train's still workable. So get it in gear!'

As the men climbed out of the jeep, Face wriggled against his binds and called out, 'We'd love to help, but . . .'

'Shut up!' Stryker cut in, wagging a finger in Peck's face.

'Any more lip outta you or your buddies and I'll gag you with your own socks.'

Peck cringed at the image, making a sick face. 'Boy, you sure know how to hurt a guy . . .'

'Dexter!' Stryker called out, summoning his sidekick over and gesturing to Face and B.A. 'Put these two clowns in the boxcar. We'll take care of them down the line.'

As Dexter prodded his charges towards the train with the barrel of his gun, Hannibal asked Stryker, 'What about me? We going to play canasta, maybe?'

'Oh, I've got better games in store for you, chump,' Stryker said. 'First, though, we're going to take a ride back to the ranch. I'm sure Mister Carter wants to have a few words with you.'

'Wonderful, don't mind if I do,' Hannibal replied. 'I have a few words I'd like to share with him, too. Maybe we can break out the Scrabble game and have ourselves some fun.'

'Keep an eye on him if you do,' Face advised Stryker. 'Hannibal's always got a few extra tiles up his sleeve.'

As Hannibal was led past his partners toward the jeep, he told them, 'Hang in there.'

'Don't hold your breath,' Stryker said. 'There ain't no cavalry coming to your aid in this picture.'

'You keep hoping that, ace,' Hannibal said, climbing leisurely into the jeep.

Stryker got in and started up the jeep, trying not to show that he'd been unnerved by Hannibal. As he drove off, following a dirt road that ran next to the main line, he kept looking around, seeing in every bush and clump of trees a possible place of concealment for allies who were in league with Hannibal. The paranoia consumed him, and before he'd driven half a mile, he turned back and returned to the site of the skirmish, where he ordered Dexter to join him in the jeep and act as an armed guard the rest of the way back to Bent Oak Ranch. Even with an extra pair of eyes to keep a lookout, Hannibal's captors failed to notice that there were, indeed, people in the hills watching them.

Murdock, Shelly, and Daniel Running Bear were

crouched around Amy at the lip of the ledge from which they had instigated their airborne assault on the train.

'I wish there was something we could do,' Amy whispered, staring at the receding jeep. 'I feel so helpless.'

'There's plenty we can do,' Murdock resolved, rising to the occasion and shucking his leisure instability in favour of heroic posturings. Rising to his feet, he pointed to his horse, which he'd retrieved at dawn from the stables so that the A-Team could have some mode of transport in the more treacherous reaches of the land around the tracks. 'I'll stick with Hannibal while you guys rustle up some help . . . oh, bad choice of words. Wrangle some help.'

'Rustle, wrangle, don't worry, we'll try,' Amy said. 'What about you, Murdock? Are you sure you can follow Hanni . . .'

She left the sentence dangling, because Murdock was already out of earshot, dodging across the ridgetop towards his horse. Once he'd untied it from the trunk of a small tree, he swung into the saddle with effortless finesse and reared the horse so that it kicked the air with its front hooves before springing forward and carrying Murdock from view.

'Where'd he learn to do that?' Amy wondered.

As with most closet heroes, Murdock had learned his moves from television. When one watched the real Range Rider mount a horse one thousand, seven-hundred and seventy-one times, including reruns, over a period of twenty-five years, osmosis had a way of translating the passive observance into something approximating first-hand knowledge. He'd also learned how to ride a horse from watching the tube and taking mental notes. As such, he was able to keep up with the jeep travelling below him, at the same time keeping himself beyond the view of Dexter in the vehicle's back seat – yet another special talent gleaned from active viewing. The lone flaw in Murdock's stealthy pursuit was his constant humming of the Range Rider theme song, but fortunately he was far away enough from the jeep that it didn't matter.

TWENTY-EIGHT

Fortunately for Stryker, the bad news he had to deliver to Bus Carter was cushioned substantially by a long-distance call Carter had just received from the Lugansk brothers in Kansas City. Not only had he been assured to his satisfaction that the brothers hadn't been behind the hiring of the A-Team, but to prove that the Carter-Lugansk alliance was still in fine working order, the brothers had arranged it so that Richard McGivers, the head buyer for Brand Meats, not only wrote off the service charge for the use of his two engines in delivering Carter's cattle to the Brand Stockyards, but also delivered the best price per head in over a year. Carter had, in short, manipulated his way into a profit that matched the ranch's previous nine month total for earned revenues. He'd made out like a bandit. If need be, he could have his damaged locomotive completely overhauled, even replaced, without feeling an economic pinch.

'And, for once, you nabbed the bastards instead of letting them get away,' Carter told Stryker, winding up his philosophical waxing of the day's developments. He downed the last swallow of cognac from his snifter, then smacked his lips and wrapped them around a cigar as he led Stryker from the den.

'Well, there's still that Injun on the loose, and a couple others,' Stryker admitted, 'but I think we got the important ones. I doubt that the others'll make a move without them.'

'If they do, we'll just have to deal with them, that's all,' Carter said. 'These people have to learn the meaning of ruffling my feathers.'

'You bet, Mister Carter.' Stryker held the door open and waited until Bus was out on the porch before following behind him. Hannibal was still in the jeep, which was parked in front of the ranch house.

'Well, well,' Carter chuckled, blowing a thin cloud of smoke Hannibal's way. 'If it isn't Buffalo Bill himself.'

Hannibal let the smoke envelope him, then slowly fade, refusing to even blink at the stinging sensation in his eyes. 'It wouldn't do me any good to call you any names,' he told Carter, ''cause I can't imagine there's one I could think of that you haven't been called already.'

'Sticks and stones, my friend,' Carter mused. 'Sticks and stones can break my bones, but words can never hurt me.'

'So you made it through nursery school, Carter,' Hannibal taunted. 'You rise in my estimation.'

Carter's mood changed in the short time it took him to lash out with the back of his hand, catching Hannibal across the face. 'Let me tell you something, fella. You're a lucky man you let my niece go unharmed, or I wouldn't have any mercy on you. Since you did, though, I'm not going to make you die slowly like I planned originally.'

'Oh, really?' Hannibal said, unperturbed. 'Wanna know something funny? I met this guy on the street in LA the other week, and he told me I *was* dying slowly already. He said we *all* are dying slowly. Real downer, huh?'

During the exchange between Hannibal and Carter, Stryker had put a quick call through to Jake, checking on the progress with the train. Flicking off the two-way radio, he told Carter, 'Babtany says they figure to be back on the main line in less than half an hour. He's checked over the engine and he's pretty sure it'll stand up to a trip across the border and back.'

'Half hour, eh?' Carter stroked his chin, lost in thought. 'That should give you just enough time to get the mustangs out of the corral and herded down to the train. I want them out of my hair today!'

'I don't know if I'd do that if I were you, Carter,' Hannibal interrupted. 'I mean, that's a long way to go with the stallions out in the open for folks to see from the road.

Somebody might get curious as to why you've got – '

'Did I ask for your opinion?' Carter demanded. 'You think I'd be stupid enough to run 'em in sight of the road? Don't be an idiot. There's half a dozen other ways to the train. Nobody's gonna spot me and, who knows, maybe we can round up a few more of the horses on the way there?'

'You want me to take the north pass then, boss?' Stryker asked.

Carter nodded. 'Tell Jesse to fire up my bird, too. I think I'll shoot along with you, make sure things go without a hitch.' Casting Hannibal a sidelong glance, he added, 'Maybe I'll get a chance to take a few pot shots at the folks that got away. I'm a pretty fair shot from the air, wouldn't you say, Stryker?'

'I'd say you're better than fair, Mister Carter.'

Hannibal smirked at Stryker, 'And I thought that brown around your nose was a moustache.'

Enraged, Stryker made a move to strike Hannibal, but Carter intercepted him. 'Now, now, Phil, don't let a condemned man rile you. You should feel privileged that he spoke his last words to you.'

Eddie Dexter had been sitting in the rear of the jeep all along, managing his lifelong speciality of being inconspicuous. When Carter looked at him and gave him an impression of someone applying a gag, Dexter grabbed Hannibal's bandana and used it to bind the prisoner's mouth in a position that made speaking difficult and eloquence impossible. When Hannibal rebelled by trying to jump from the jeep, Dexter grabbed him by the collar and jerked him back into his seat.

'What do you want me to do with him, Mister Carter?'

Carter told Dexter, 'Take him out and use him to fertilize the south forty.'

'Gladly,' Dexter said.

As Dexter was bounding out of the jeep and circling around to the driver's side, Carter and Stryker headed off in the direction of the stables and the helipad. Before they went their separate ways at the barn, Carter told his foreman, 'Okay, let's do this quick, while Lane's still nappin'. We're just lucky she hasn't wandered near enough to the stables since she's been here, or she'd know about the mustangs already.'

Even as Carter was speaking, his niece was less than twenty feet away from him, hiding inside the door of the barn, where she'd been playing with one of the puppies just born to the ranch hound. She'd overheard the entire conversation between Hannibal and his three tormentors, and she was in shock over her uncle's cold-heartedness. Unwilling to confront him on the spot, she held her breath and withdrew even further from the doorway as Carter walked past. She was holding onto the puppy, and when it began to whine in her arms, she quickly bent over and let it go. The puppy immediately scampered between her legs and behind her. As she turned to watch it, a hand suddenly clamped itself on her mouth and slowly turned her head to meet its owner.

'Shhhhhhh,' Howling Mad Murdock whispered. 'Now that your uncle's blown the whistle on himself, are you still gonna make believe we're the bad guys around here?'

Lane shook her head, breathing heavily through her nose as Murdock continued to hold a hand over her mouth.

'Good, because I'm going to need a favour from you.' When Lane bobbed affirmatively, Murdock asked her, 'If I take my hand away, you're not going to scream for help, are you?'

Lane shook her head again. Murdock held up his end of the bargain and let go of her. Dabbing at her lips, Carter's niece asked, 'What do you want me to do?'

'I want you to count to ten, *then* scream for help.'

'Why?'

'Don't ask questions. The Range Rider always has his reasons.'

'Well . . . okay. Ten . . . nine . . . eight . . . seven . . .'

Murdock stole quickly across the barn and slipped out the side door, counting to himself in time with Lane. His horse was tethered between the side door and a large corn crib, shielding it from view to anyone passing by the barn. As he climbed into the saddle, he heard the distant sound of

Carter's helicopter whirring into life. 'Five . . . four . . . this is it, Mr Ed Thunder,' he told his horse, bracing for the end of the countdown. 'Two, one, and we're off!'

Lane's scream rang out on schedule, making it sound as if she'd gone into the barn to play with a puppy and had ended up facing a stray pack of rabid dobermans. When Dexter heard the woman, he immediately stopped the jeep and looked around, trying to place where the scream had come from. Hannibal was as in the dark as Dexter about what was happening, but he didn't waste time worrying about it. He saw the distraction for what it was, and capitalized on it. Pivoting about as best as he could in his seat, he lashed out with his right foot and kicked Dexter out of the jeep. The ranch hand took the move unprepared, and landed sprawling in the dirt, one wrist sprained from trying to break his fall. As he spouted obscenities and clambered back to his feet, Hannibal rolled out of the other side of the vehicle and fought his own battle for balance as he sought out his likeliest avenue of escape. He spotted Lane waving at him from the barn at roughly the same time Dexter managed to get his gun out and draw aim at him.

'Oh, no you don't!' Murdock forewarned Dexter as his horse bore down on the unsuspecting flunky, who whirled around just in time for Murdock to slip his foot from his stirrup and plant it in the other man's chest, knocking the wind from his lungs and sending him spinning back to the ground, gasping for air.

Lane rushed over and removed Hannibal's gag.

'Good show, Murdock!' Hannibal cheered as he waited for Lane to unfasten the rest of his binds.

'Were they really going to kill you?' Lane asked.

'I think that was the general idea,' Hannibal admitted. 'Sorry to take the sheep's clothing off your uncle, but I think at least you can see him for what he is . . .'

'Yes, I can,' she said, shame in her voice. 'Can you stop them from having the horses taken to Mexico?'

'That's the next item on our agenda,' Hannibal said, rubbing his chaffed wrists as he looked over at where Murdock was trying to show off on his horse. Rearing the stallion, he raised clenched fists over his head in a gesture of victory more befitting Sylvester Stallone as Rock Balboa than Howling Mad Murdock as the Range Rider, especially when performed on horseback. One moment he was a picture of triumph, the next he looked for all the world like a rodeo clown, tumbling awkwardly from his horse and landing in a heap next to Dexter, who was still incapacitated.

'Come on, Rider,' Hannibal shouted, breaking away from Lane and running to the jeep. He started up the engine and spun around as Murdock leapt into the back. As the two of them rode off, they both waved, Hannibal to Lane and Murdock to Mr Ed Thunder, his trusty steed.

TWENTY-NINE

The land rover Daniel was driving had been put through far less trying road tests than the punishment the Indian was subjecting it to as he sought out the quickest passageway through the wilderness that could be managed without raising the telltale clouds of dust he would have left in his wake had he stuck to the dirt roads. Amy and Shelly clung to their seats as the rover bounded over rock-strewn strips of land and scaled treacherous inclines.

'I think we should strike out for Ohigai once we get the chance,' Amy shouted above the engine's fierce revving. 'We're going to have to bring the sheriff into this.'

'The sheriff?' Daniel questioned, negotiating a hairpin turn around a swollen boulder. 'I thought your friends were wanted by the military police and that there were some officers at the sheriff's office only yesterday . . .'

'Well, do you have any better ideas? We can't count on Murdock pulling off a miracle, and the three of us aren't in a position to spring B.A. and Face by ourselves.'

'Why not?' Shelly ventured from the back seat. 'All I need are some more arrows and some more dynamite and I – '

'Forget it, Shelly,' Daniel said. 'I think we should try swinging by the reservation.'

'What for?' Amy asked.

'Maybe I can get a bunch of the guys to come on out and help.'

'If they wouldn't help before, what makes you think they would now?' Amy countered. 'We can't afford the risk of wasting that much time. Let's get into town and see the sheriff. My first worry is keeping the guys from getting killed. If they get taken into custody afterwards . . . well, Hannibal can always come up with a way to escape.'

Daniel thought it over, then promptly changed directions and headed down a slope of wild grass and scattered oaks. 'I think you're right. It would have been Hannibal's way of thinking, at any rate . . .'

After following the downgrade for a quarter of a mile, Daniel veered to the east, finally coming back in contact with one of the dirt roads that combed the hills between Ohigai and the reservation. Taking the route leading into town, Daniel had to pass through a long stretch of roadway flanked on one side by a precipitous dropoff and on the other by an abrupt rise every bit as steep as the cliff near the site where the A-Team had bushwhacked Carter's train the first time. The roadway was little more than a lane and a half wide, making it next to impossible to turn around. Daniel realized as much even before he saw the approach of two unmarked sedans racing up from town.

'The MPs!' Amy gasped.

'I was afraid of that. Hold onto your hats, gang.' Daniel braked the land rover a dozen yards short of the sedans, which spread out, one behind the other, in such a way as to block the entire road. As the doors to the sedans swung open and several officers piled out, brandishing weapons, Daniel shifted into reverse and looked over his shoulder as he began backing the land rover up as fast as he possibly could.

It wasn't fast enough.

Nine shots echoed in the air as three officers directed their fire at the retreating vehicle. The majority of them found their mark, puncturing the rover's radiator, front tyres, and otherwise desecrating the front end. Steam boiled out of the radiator as the vehicle sank forward on the rims of its front wheels.

'Stop where you are and nobody has to get hurt!' Colonel Decker shouted at the threesome in the disabled car.

'Should we level with them?' Daniel whispered to Amy. 'It'd save us the trouble of hunting down the sheriff.'

'I don't think we have a choice,' Amy said. 'I was hoping we could just deal with the locals, but this'll have to do. We just can't make it look like we're asking them for favours or they're apt to go ahead and let Carter get rid of the guys for him.'

'Gotcha,' Daniel said as Decker and three other men, including Lieutenant Crane, headed for the rover. Glancing back at Shelly, he advised, 'And no smart remarks out of you, okay?'

Shelly nodded.

'How lucky for me to run into you like this,' Decker told the trio, grinning maliciously.

'I don't understand,' Daniel said.

'Oh, you understand, all right,' Decker said, 'Otherwise you wouldn't have been in such a hurry to run away from us like you did.'

'I don't know what you're talking about,' Daniel insisted. 'Look, we have lots of problems with drunks from town coming up into the hills to give my people problems. When you blocked the road, I thought it meant trouble. Who are you anyway?'

'We'll get to that in good time,' Decker replied. 'In the meantime, are you Daniel Running Bear?'

'What makes you ask?'

'Your licence plate . . . and I have a description of your vehicle. I'm Colonel Decker of the US Army. I've been trying to reach you at your home all day. I finally decided to drive out to speak with you. Good thing or we might have missed each other again.'

'And what was it you wanted to see me about?' Daniel asked warily. 'I served my time in Nam and got an honourable discharge. My nose has been clean all the years since and – '

'I'm not much interested in you, actually,' Decker said. 'I'm looking for some people you ran around with during your last trip to LA. I want to know where the A-Team is.'

'The A-Team?'

'Yes, that's right.' Decker said. 'I know they're in the area, but I want something a little more specific.'

'Well, I sure wish I could help you, officer, but – '

'If you can't help me, Daniel,' Decker interrupted,

shifting his heartless gaze to Amy, 'I'm sure Miss Allen here can.'

Amy pretended to be startled. 'Why, how did you know who I was?'

'It's my job to know, lady. I also know that you have a tendency to be around whenever the A-Team turns up anywhere. You know, you have a lot in common with Clark Kent. I mean, you're both reporters and you both have this knack of – '

'Spare me, would you, Colonel?' Amy said. 'I'm here on assignment from the Courier-Express. I've got notes and photos in my car, and if you'll let me make a phone call, I'm sure we can straighten this all out.'

Decker signalled to Crane and the other officers, who circled around either side of the land rover to apprehend the three riders within. 'I'm sorry, Miss Allen but you've been, shall we say, reassigned? . . .'

THIRTY

The scarred locomotive was back on the main line, belching steam and smoke as it waited for the call to roll. As Jake dutifully inspected the engine for leaks, Stryker and Carter oversaw the coaxing of the last few stallions up the ramp leading into the boxcar.

'Train took quite a shelling, all right,' Carter told his foreman. 'I wonder if I should even bother trying to come up with a cover story for my insurance broker.'

'Vandals,' Stryker suggested. 'Tell him it was vandals that did it.'

'I might do just that.' Carter moved away from the boxcar as its door was being slid into place. 'For now, I'll be glad just to get these horses out of my sight, along with the rest of these troublemakers.'

Reaching the coal car, both men climbed up the ladder and glanced into the hold, where Face and B.A. had been transferred to make room for the horses. A layer of coal dust had already settled over them, making them look like understudies for Amos and Andy.

'Lucky boys, you get to travel first-class,' Carter quipped, pulling three cigars from his coat pocket. He put one in his mouth, and offered the others to Face and B.A. 'I hate to say it, but we won't be showing movies, since you'll be getting off so soon. As a gesture of hospitality, though, here's a sampling of the finest tobaccos Havana has to offer. What's an execution without a last smoke, I always say.'

'That's real swell of you,' Face said, opening his mouth to accept the cigar. 'Hannibal always told me I didn't know what I was missing. Now I get to find out. Much obliged.'

B.A. said nothing. Once the cigar was between his lips,

he chewed it down to a quick pulp and spat it out at Carter and Stryker. 'I'd do the same to you if I wasn't tied up, sucker!'

'You shouldn't have done that,' Stryker said, taking a step back to the ladder. 'Now I'm afraid your friend isn't going to be able to have me light *his* cigar.'

'That's okay,' Face said. 'Knowing you, Carter, it'd probably blow up in my face.'

Carter laughed. 'Oh, that would have been a nice touch. I wish I would have thought of it.'

'There's a lot you haven't thought of, Carter,' Face said.

Stryker took a threatening step towards Face, at the same time asking Carter, 'You want I should gag 'em?'

'No need to bother,' Carter said, starting down the ladder. 'Once the train's rolling, they can yell all they want and nobody's going to hear it.'

Jake was waiting for Carter when he climbed down. 'Ready any time you are, Mister Carter.'

Carter put a hand on the engineer's shoulder and looked him in the eye. 'I know this has been hard on you, Jake, and that you've been keeping a stiff upper lip about it all. I want you to know that once you're back from Mexico, I'll see to it that you have everything you need to get ol' Abigail here back to her old self.'

A smile crept across Jake's face. 'I really do appreciate that, Mister Carter.'

'My pleasure. Now get going . . . and make sure that once you cross the border, Stryker takes care of those yahoos in the coal bin.'

'You don't have to worry about them being taken care of, Mister Carter,' Jake promised.

'Good, good.'

Carter stepped back from the train and watched as Jake climbed up into the engine to take over the controls. The train whistle sounded, more jets of steam shot out from the sides of the locomotive, then the wheels began to turn.

'Happy Trails,' Carter called out, waving to Jake and Stryker. Once the train was well on its way, the ranch owner ordered his men to ride back to the Bent Oak to catch up on the errands that had fallen to the wayside during the commotion of the past few days. As countless hooves beat a din into the midday air, Carter strolled over to where his pilot was still seated inside the cockpit of his private helicopter, engrossed in a paperback novel.

'Hey, Jesse! Toss that crap aside and get this bird ready for liftoff!' Carter shouted, pausing fifty yards from the helicopter to savour the last few puffs of his cigar. As the rotors began to spin and pick up momentum, stirring dustclouds all around the chopper, Carter watched the train roll past the Southwest-Mexicali Salvage Yard and disappear around the next bend, leaving a thin trail of smoke lingering in its wake.

Just then the drone of another motor impinged upon Carter's threshold of hearing. Cocking his head to one side, he placed the sound and turned around to look behind him.

'What the hell!!??'

With Hannibal behind the wheel, one of Carter's own jeeps was swinging around a corner and racing toward the helicopter, with Murdock riding beside him, donning his coveted mask.

Throwing down what was left of his cigar, Carter hurried to the helicopter, crouching forward to stay low of the rotor's sweeping arc. 'Get this up!' he screamed at Jesse as he struggled aboard.

Jesse, a gaunt-looking cowpoke with a fetish for leather outfits, pulled back on his control stick, achieving lift-off. However, Hannibal was able to stop the jeep and rush out in time to catch hold of one of the chopper's skids. Murdock, with a spurt of agility that would have made his mentor proud, managed to jump the other skid, slowing down the copter's ascent and forcing Jesse to concentrate fully on keeping the machine from crashing.

Carter tried to keep Hannibal from the cockpit by swinging the door open into the Colonel's face. Hannibal was able to duck the anticipated blow, then throw himself in at Carter, subduing the land baron before he could make use of the .22 he'd yanked out of his pocket.

'Always playing with that gun, aren't you, Carter?'

Hannibal said, taking the weapon away and pointing it at Jesse. 'As for you, my friend, you don't mind if my personal pilot takes over, do you?'

'If I don't bring this bird under control, we're all going to be dead meat!' Jesse shouted, frantically working the controls.

'Oh, I don't know about that,' Hannibal said as Murdock opened the pilot's door to the cockpit. 'I think if we shed a few pounds, things'll work out just fine . . .'

Jesse turned out to be the few pounds Hannibal had in mind. As Hannibal pushed the gun in Jesse's face and ordered him to relinquish the controls, Murdock grabbed the pilot and perfunctorily ejected him from the aircraft. They were less than twenty feet above the ground, so Jesse landed in a less-than-fatal heap as Murdock slipped into the pilot's seat and quickly brought the helicopter under control.

'Well done, Range Rider,' Hannibal congratulated Murdock.

'T'weren't nothin',' Murdock scoffed.

'Now let's go find ourselves that train!'

As Murdock veered the copter about, Hannibal grabbed a length of cable from the floor between his feet and turned to Carter, who was eyeing him venomously.

'You bastards!'

'Easy, now, Carter, or we'll send you down to hike back to the ranch with your pilot,' Hannibal warned. 'Of course, now we're about a hundred feet up and you don't have a parachute . . . think about it while I put these bracelets on. They should hold you until we can fit you with something sturdier at the nearest house of correction . . .'

THIRTY-ONE

'How many miles to the border?' Stryker asked Jake.

'I figure about eight.'

'And how's Abigail holdin' up?'

Jake inspected the gauges monitoring the engine's vital signs. 'She's not complaining too much, considering what she's been through.' Jake cast a glance back at the two prisoners in the coal tender. 'Say, Phil, once we cross the border, how about if you let me take care of these guys? It'd make me feel a whole lot better.'

'Well, I don't rightly know, Jake. I got a few things to settle with them myself.'

'Maybe we'll split 'em up, then. One man apiece.'

'Sounds fair to me. I think I'd like the one with . . .'

'What is it, Phil? Why'd you just stop right in the – '

'Shhhhhh, listen!' Stryker said, moving to the cab window. 'Hear that?'

Jake strained his ears, trying to filter out the sounds of his beloved Abigail. Finally he sorted out the one noise that wasn't coming from the train. Stepping to the other window, he poked his head out and looked up. 'I'll be jiggered. It's Mister Carter's chopper. Why d'ya figure he decided to follow us?'

'Maybe he doesn't trust us to finish off the job right,' Stryker speculated, 'You know how he gets . . . no, wait, wait a second! Look, somebody's gettin' out!'

As the helicopter swerved down closer to the train, Jake and Stryker were able to see that it was Hannibal who had climbed out onto one of the skids.

'I sure as hell don't know how he got up there,' Stryker said, reaching for his gun, 'but I aim to help him get down.'

Murdock brought the chopper directly over the train, then matched his speed with that of Abigail as Hannibal dangled by his hands from the skids, getting ready to jump once he had a good bead on the roof of the boxcar. Two shots whistling past his head disrupted his concentration some, but he finally dropped, lighting on the section of roof that had been spared from Shelly's explosive arrow earlier in the day.

'Damn!' Stryker swore. 'Jake, keep this mother going, hear? Don't stop, no matter what!'

'But, Jake, what about – '

'Just do what I say! I'm goin' after him!'

Gun in hand, Stryker entered the coal tender, snarling at Face and B.A. as he stalked past them and started climbing up the pile of fuel. By the time he reached the rim and peered over it, hoping to get a clear shot at Hannibal before the A-Team's leader had had a chance to regain his balance, he found that he was too late. Hannibal was gone. Stryker quickly looked off to the side of the tracks to see if he'd fallen off the boxcar, but Hannibal was nowhere to be seen. Swinging his gun down at the couplings, Stryker saw that Hannibal wasn't between the two railcars, either.

'He's gotta be behind the car,' Stryker figured to himself, taking a cautious leap onto the roof of the boxcar. There was a large, long gash in the roof, through which he could see inside the boxcar. The mustangs were restless, moving nervously about and neighing loudly.

Once Stryker was out of their view, B.A. and Face shuffled until they were back to back, enabling them, however awkwardly, to attempt to untie each other's binds. It was a frustrating challenge, and the urgency of their situation didn't help matters any.

'Will you stay still?' Face hissed, keeping an eye on Jake as he fingered B.A.'s knots. The engineer had his back turned to them, busying himself with adjusting a temperamental lever that kept popping out of position.

'I am staying still, man!' B.A. insisted. 'It's the train that's moving!'

'Oh, that's rich, B.A. Keep up the comedy; I could use a

good laugh about now . . .'

'Hold it, I think I got this knot!' B.A. grimaced as he contorted his hands, trying to give Peck's rope a good tug. When he did, the knot loosened to the point where Face could wriggle his wrists free from bondage.

'Good goin', B.A.!' Peck quickly returned the favour, untying B.A. as he asked, 'What's our plan now?'

B.A. checked to make sure Jake was still preoccupied with his repairs, then said, 'See if you can pop the pin holdin' us to the engine. I wanna check and see how Hannibal's doin' . . .'

As Peck advanced slowly towards the front of the coal tender and B.A. stole up the black slope of the fuel heap, Murdock was watching them from overhead. To further ensure that Jake wouldn't look behind him and see that the prisoners were on the loose, Murdock eased the helicopter forward and held a constant speed that kept him hovering constantly in view just above the front end of the locomotive.

Reaching the coupling between the engine and the coal car, Peck braced himself and pulled hard on the pin. It was securely fixed in place and the tension from moving made it even harder to work free. Blood began to trickle from painful scrapes Peck suffered trying to get a firm grip on the pin, and he was already drained from the physical ordeals he had been through in the past few days. But somewhere in his system there was a small reserve of adrenalin, and he called upon it to give one last, valiant tug on the pin. It popped loose in his hand, and immediately a gap appeared between the engine and tender, widening by the second as Abigail steamed on towards the not-too-distant border. The coal car and the boxcar behind continued to roll by the force of their own momentum, though, and it was clear to Face that they would reach the upcoming bend that dipped down at an angle that seemed sufficient enough to ensure that both cars would roll all the way into Mexico without help of the engine.

At the moment Face had pulled the coupling pin, Stryker had crept to the far end of the roof and was about to lean over and take a potshot at Hannibal, who was clinging, unarmed, to the ladder affixed to the rear of the boxcar. The sudden shift in speed, however, threw Stryker's balance off, and he staggered a few steps backwards, holding his arms out as he tried to regain his equilibrium. Hannibal swiftly cleared the upper rungs of the ladder and hurled himself across the roof, tackling Stryker with the certainty of a defensive end bringing down an elusive quarterback trying an end sweep. Stryker went down hard, and his gun clattered over the edge of the roof.

'Hand-to-hand's good enough for me!' Stryker spat, breaking free of Hannibal's grip and rolling away. Both men rose to their feet, balancing themselves like surfers against the shifting of the runaway boxcar as they closed in on one another.

'I'll warn you, I'm a stunt man,' Hannibal said. 'I'm used to this sort of thing.'

'Yeah? I've had rougher times getting around after a few drinks than this,' Stryker boasted, making a few feints Hannibal's way and lashing out with his hand, trying to shove the other man. Hannibal leaned away from each blow, all the while inching closer to his foe. However, the need for concentration on Stryker's every move prevented Hannibal from taking a good look at the roof beneath him. He took one step in the wrong direction and inadvertently twisted his ankle on a spot where dynamite had ripped a hole. Reeling to one side, the only way Hannibal saved himself from falling off the roof was by catching his fingers on the same hole that had tripped him up. As it was, though, his legs dangled over the sides of the boxcar and he had only one hand free to fend off any move Stryker might make.

'Tough break, pal,' Stryker taunted, moving over and staying out of Hannibal's reach. 'I think I got something stuck to the bottom of my boot. I'm sure you won't mind if I scrape it off on the back of your hand . . .'

Stryker was about to crush Hannibal's fingers under the sole of his right boot when he suddenly felt himself being jerked backwards. B.A. had come up from behind and grabbed Stryker, spinning him around and asking, 'You mind if I polish my rings on your face, sucker?'

Without waiting for permission, B.A. went ahead and introduced his right fist to Stryker's jaw. The foreman crumpled under the force of the punch, and B.A. helped ease him down onto the roof so he wouldn't topple off, then went over to lend Hannibal a hand.

'Thanks, B.A.,' Hannibal groaned as he climbed back up onto the roof. 'I owe you a big one for that.'

'You wanna pay me back, find a way to stop this thing!' B.A. said, moving along to the next obstacle facing the A-Team.

Hannibal looked ahead and saw the incline they were approaching. Less than a mile down the line, their locomotive was still barrelling ahead at full steam. 'Well, so much for asking Jake pretty please to put the brakes on . . .'

'Brakes!' Peck called out, vaulting from the coal tender to the boxcar. 'There should be a manual wheel somewhere at the back end of this thing.'

The men headed back to the ladder Hannibal had held onto before his confrontation with Stryker. Next to the bottom rung and left of the unused coupling was the brake wheel Peck had been talking about. Hannibal was the first one down the ladder, followed by Peck. The two of them took turns trying to budge the wheel, but it proved to be even more obstinate than the coupling pin Face had dealt with moments before.

'It's all yours, B.A.,' Hannibal said when Baracus joined them on the narrow platform surrounding the wheel.

As Hannibal and Peck moved aside to give B.A. room, Peck mused, 'Too bad I didn't bring my special grease.'

'That's okay,' Hannibal said. 'I have confidence in B.A.'s elbow grease.'

Gritting his teeth, B.A. put his full weight into the wheel, trying to wrestle it clockwise. When he received no results, he tried the other way, with equal failure.

'Where's Murdock?' Face said, scanning the sky. 'Maybe he can come pluck us up.'

'And leave these horses to crash land . . . after all we've

gone through to help 'em? No way,' Hannibal said. 'Come on, B.A., you can do it!'

'I'm tryin', man!' B.A. grunted, breaking out in a sweat as he continued to apply pressure on the wheel. At last he was able to get it to turn. The high-pitched shriek of steel chaffing against steel became louder and more persistent as he moved it more, and the boxcar began to quake and rattle, slowing down in sporadic bursts. Hannibal and Face crowded in next to B.A., and they all took turns at the brake until it had succeeded in locking the wheels of the boxcar completely, ending their flight a good hundred feet before the start of the incline. With the brakes and wheels silenced, there was only the restless sounds of the horses to compete with the exhausted gasps of relief by the three men gathered around the brake wheel. They looked at one another, grateful to be alive.

'Boy!' Face sighed, cracking his winsome grin, 'That was almost – '

'Don't say it,' Hannibal cut in, to no avail.

'– the end of the line,' Face and B.A. muttered in unison.

THIRTY-TWO

Once he'd seen that Peck had been able to undo the coupling pin connecting the coal tender to the locomotive, Murdock had kept the helicopter lingering in Jake's field of vision a few seconds longer, then swung away from the train and headed back to see if he could be of any assistance to his companions on the freed cars. Before he could complete the arc of his sweeping turn, he spotted something off in the distance that begged for closer inspection. Two clouds of dust were scudding down the road leading from the hills, and the closer he drew to them, the more he was able to discern the vehicles responsible for the phenomena.

'Oh oh . . .' Murdock mumbled, leaning on the controls to change the chopper's course. 'Looks like the Range Rider's arch-nemeses, the Black Rock gang themselves, have shown up for a showdown . . .'

'What the hell are you babbling about?' Carter demanded, squirming about the back of the chopper, trying to shake his binds. 'Do you know what the penalty is for kidnapping?'

'Who's nappin' kids? I thought it was mustangs you were grabbin'. Penalty for that's stiff, might stiff . . .'

'Me! You're kidnapping *me*, you ignorant fool!' Carter railed. 'Look, I own the law in these parts. I can make it rough or easy on you, depending on the way you want it. Think it over . . .'

As he jockeyed the controls and flew back to where B.A. and the others were slowing down the runaway cars, Murdock sat tall in his seat and declared, 'Mister, you may think you *own* the law in these parts, but the Range Rider *is* the law in these parts, and he's not for sale!'

'Name your price!' Carter bartered. 'How does fifteen thousand dollars grab you? I've got that much in another safe back at the ranch. Cold, hard cash. All you have to do it take me there to get it and it's all yours.'

Murdock saw that the two military sedans were heading straight for where the A-Team had sidetracked the train that morning. They were less than two miles from the stopped cars by the time Murdock brought the helicopter down on the pad of land closest to the tracks where his friends had just hopped down from the boxcar. As he kept the engine running, he pointed Carter's own .22 at him.

'Okay, mister, you convinced me. I can't go through with this kidnapping. Get out . . .'

'What?'

Murdock untied the cords tied around Carter's ankles, but left the land baron's hands bound behind his back. 'You heard me. Out. Bye bye. Hasta la pasta. You's a free man now.'

'But this isn't what I had in mind . . .' Carter stalled, looking out and seeing B.A., Peck, and Hannibal walking towards the helicopter.

'I'm picking up three men and there's only room for four here,' Murdock said. 'You got the short straw, Mister Carter. You'll just have to get out and wait for the next ride, that's all there is to it.'

When Carter still refrained from heading for the door, Murdock secured his seat belt and suddenly lifted off, tilting the copter so far to one side that Carter tumbled under the pull of gravity and almost fell out of the passenger door when it swung open beneath him.

'Out!' Murdock shouted, his eyes filled with a sudden flash of menace.

The helicopter was now hovering at more than a forty-five degree angle, and Carter saw that they were suspended above the coal car, which lay a dozen feet away.

'I said to get out!' Murdock screamed, firing the .22 so that a bullet smashed through the bubble of glass behind Carter. The rancher needed no further incentive. He jumped clumsily from the chopper and landed harshly amidst the chunks of coal, howling in pain from the force of his fall. Murdock quickly flew back to the clearing and brought the copter down.

'C'mon, c'mon!' he shouted out at the others above the sound of the rotors, which stirred up their own great cloud of dust. 'We got a bogie on the right . . . certified trouble!'

Hannibal, Peck, and B.A. looked off in the distance and saw the two sedans speeding towards them. There could be no mistaking the meaning.

'Man, this new guy's got Lynch beat all to hell,' B.A. snorted, bending over and rushing to the helicopter. Face followed suit, leaving Hannibal to stand and watch the cars loom closer into view.

'C'mon, Hannibal, let's go!' Face cried out, following B.A. into the helicopter.

But instead of rushing to join them, Hannibal stood his ground and leisurely plucked a cigar from his pocket. 'They're not close enough to see it's us,' he commented.

'Are you crazy?' Face screamed.

Hannibal grinned. 'If this new colonel didn't get to see how close he came to topping Lynch and nabbing us . . . well, I just wouldn't be able to sleep tonight, that's all.'

This logic was lost on the others. In unison, they all bade, 'Hannibal!!!!!'

As Hannibal was lighting his cigar, the two sedans drew close enough for several officers to roll down their windows and lean out, firing shots in the direction of the helicopter. Satisfied that he'd tempted fate enough for one day, Hannibal ducked and sprinted to the chopper, bounding up the skid and into the cockpit just as Murdock was lifting off.

'Buzz 'em, Murdock!' Hannibal encouraged his pilot.

'Glad to, Colonel,' Murdock pushed the stick forward and the helicopter responded in kind, sweeping over the hoods of both sedans, taking the armed officers within by surprise. They took a few wild shots at the airborne members of the A-Team, who waved joyfully at Amy and Daniel, who were riding in the back seat of the lead vehicle.

'I knew they could do it,' Amy whispered to Daniel as she waved back at the men in the helicopter.

Both sedans ground to a halt and the military police sprang out into the open, sending a last, futile round of gunshot at the retreating helicopter. Colonel Decker emptied his revolver in frustration, then slowly lowered it, letting the bitter realization of failure begin to settle over him. Lieutenant Crane stood next to him, equally numbed.

Daniel Running Bear moved out of the sedan, followed by Amy and Shelly. They approached Crane and Decker, and pointed past the officers at the idled railcars, where Bus Carter was struggling to crawl out of the coal tender, covered with soot.

'Gentlemen,' Daniel told the officers, 'I think you'd be interested to know that boxcar is being used to illegally transport wild mustangs from reservation land.'

'I do believe that's a federal offence,' Amy added, 'And I also believe the man behind it all is right over there, ready to turn himself in.'

Decker was only half-listening to Amy and Daniel. His eyes were still on the helicopter, now little more than a speck heading off in the direction of the Mexican border, beyond range of prosecution.

'Next time, Hannibal Smith,' he vowed, his jaw clenched with determination. 'Next time . . .'

EPILOGUE

The following morning, when Daniel drove his land rover back to the reservation from the repair shop in Ohigai, followed by Amy in her convertible, they found the A-Team waiting for them.

'What are you guys doing here!?' Amy gasped, pulling to a stop next to her male associates. 'Crane's got an all-points bulletin out for that helicopter you flew off in, not to mention a tidy reward on every one of your heads!'

'Well, the helicopter's resting at the bottom of a lake just across the border,' Hannibal said nonchalantly, puffing his ever-present cigar. 'As for us, well, here we are . . .'

'We had to walk all the way here,' B.A. said. 'Beats flying with that maniac Murdock, at least.'

'I sank the chopper on orders, I'll have you know,' Murdock defended himself to Amy.

'You coulda dropped us off on land first, at least, sucker!'

'B.A., Murdock,' Hannibal mediated, 'you've been at each other's throats over that since it happened. Drop it already, all right?'

From behind the wheel of his rover, Daniel called out, 'Amy and I were just going for a ride out into the hills for a look at the mustangs. Why don't we all go?'

'I'm beat,' Face groaned. 'Maybe another time.'

Just then Shelly raced up to the group, his eyes wide with anxiety as he shouted, 'Dan'l! Them military guys are here waitin' to talk to you again. I said you were runnin' errands, then split. When I snuck back I saw 'em goin' into your place to snoop around.'

'Probably setting bugs,' Hannibal guessed, looking over at Daniel. 'They're hoping we'll be in touch through you and tip ourselves off.'

'Suddenly I'm not so tired any more,' Face said. 'Maybe we should take that little trip after all, guys.'

'I think so,' Hannibal said.

'I ain't goin' if we all gotta cram into the convertible!' B.A. declared.

'I've got room for four,' Daniel reminded B.A.

Amy, Shelly, and Murdock joined Daniel in the rover, while Face drove the convertible with Hannibal riding shotgun, leaving B.A. with the entire back seat to himself. Departing as quickly as possible to avoid a possible run-in with the MPs, they proceeded into the surrounding wilderness, making their way to the same ridgeline where the A-Team had first seen the mustangs and decided to take on the assignment that was now almost behind them.

It hadn't taken the liberated horses long to rejoin their herd and revert back to their capering ways. Down in the valley, the majority of the mustangs carried on with wild, dynamic majesty, romping playfully amidst the cotton-woods. Some grazed tranquilly on the tall grasses, while others lazed in the shade and a few lapped up water from a thin creek that wound its way across the valley floor.

'Look at them,' Amy said admiringly, not bothering with pictures this time. 'It's like they know they're not being hunted any more.'

'How great to be free,' Daniel remarked.

'Speaking of which,' Hannibal said, 'We still need to find a way out of here before Colonel Decker figures out we're still in the neighbourhood.'

'Why don't you take my convertible?' Amy suggested. 'I'm, uh, going to stay on here a while longer, anyway.'

'Still working on that background material, eh, Amy?' Face said.

'Something like that,' Amy said with a smirk.

'Seems to me I remember you saying you didn't trust us in your car, Amy,' Hannibal drawled. 'Why the change of mind?'

'I guess I just realized that being part of a team requires sacrifices sometimes. Besides, if I stay here awhile, I can help throw Decker off your scent. You know, let slip a few red herrings when I think they're eavesdropping. Things like that.'

'How noble,' Face said. 'And how do you feel about all this, Daniel?'

'It's fine by me.' From the look in the Indian's eyes as he glanced at Amy, it was clear he was telling the truth.

They watched the horses a while longer, then Hannibal said, 'Well, if we're going, I think there's no time like the present.'

'Wait!' Shelly cried out, rushing back to the land rover. He reached into the trunk and pulled out his bow, which he'd left in there the day before. Bringing it back to the group, he told B.A., 'Here, it's for you . . . you know, so you can show it to the kids at the centre. It'll help 'em better to see how to make one.'

Accepting the gift, B.A. unleashed one of his rare grins. 'Thanks, little brother. I'm sure they'll really appreciate that.'

'Okay,' Hannibal announced, 'Let's hit it!'

As the A-Team headed back to the convertible, Murdock said, 'Daniel, would you say goodbye to Ed for me?'

'Sure, Murdock.'

Murdock climbed into the back seat with Face, still troubled. When Amy and Daniel walked over with Shelly to send them off, he said, 'Ah, Daniel . . . could you tell him if he ever needs me . . . if he feels the need to talk and there's no one else around, well . . . I'll always lend an ear.'

'That's good,' B.A. scoffed from the front seat, ''cause you ain't got no brain to loan, that's for sure!'

'Good luck,' Daniel wished the A-Team.

'Send me a postcard,' Amy wisecracked.

B.A. started up the convertible and pulled out. All four men in the car offered a final wave, then vanished around the first bend leading down from the ridge. Daniel turned and glanced back down at the valley floor, where the mustangs continued to roam.

'They really did it,' he said softly.

'They always do,' Amy told him, her voice ringing with pride.

'Hey, look at this!' Shelly called out, running over to pick up something from the dirt. It was Murdock's Range Rider mask. 'He musta forgot it!'

'I don't think he forgot it,' Amy ventured. 'My guess is he left it behind because his job was done.'

'Holy cow! Look what's clipped to it!'

Daniel looked and couldn't believe what he saw. 'Money!' As he began counting it, he realized, 'It's what I paid them to take the job. I don't get it.'

'I do,' Amy said, her throat tightening with emotion. 'It's just like them. Typical.'

'But I can't take this back. They worked hard. They deserve something.'

'Oh, I'm sure they got something out of all this,' Amy said.

'What's that?' Shelly asked.

'Well, Shelly, the A-Team has this saying. "We do it for the jazz . . ."'